WHERE THE DEAD GO TO DIE

AARON DRIES &
MARK ALLAN GUNNELLS

Crystal Lake Publishing
www.CrystalLakePub.com

OTHER TITLES BY ...

OTHER NOVELS BY CRYSTAL LAKE PUBLISHING

Or check out other Crystal Lake Publishing books for your Dark Fiction, Horror, Suspense, and Thriller needs, and join our newsletter while you're there.

DEDICATION

"To Anne Kelly Tromsness,
for always shining your light in the darkness."
—Mark Allan Gunnells

"I'm dedicating this book to every single amazing
aged care nurse I've worked with over the years. You
all know who you are. Next time we're together, we
can show off our scars like the three shark hunters in
JAWS, sipping on a well-earned drink, singing 'Show
Me The Way To Go Home . . . '"
—Aaron Dries

WELCOME ABOARD

"**THE DEAD ROAM** those halls."

At first, Emily assumed the voice was her own, an echo bouncing off the building's façade. She continued toward the entrance nonetheless, brushing the cliché away as though it were just another snowflake caught on her coat. Every one of her steps ushered the cinderblock structure closer until it loomed overhead, and as she passed into its shadow, Emily found herself admiring how the building managed to be both nondescript *and* foreboding at the same time, a balancing act of utilitarian blandness that screamed *government institution!*

The voice spoke again. No, not just spoke. It *came* at her.

"That place belongs to the dead."

She paused. The speaker wasn't in her head, rather somewhere to her right: an old woman with wild gray hair, dressed in black. Emily knew she shouldn't be unsettled—that she was above all the theatrical bullshit that came with this territory—yet she felt her stomach knotting anyway.

"The dead roam those halls." Repeated, of course, for emphasis. And worst of all, it fucking worked.

"I know."

The old woman's expression was pinched into a familiar mask of fear and desperation. *Familiar, yes*—but from where? Emily clutched her coat, though the chill rippling through her nerve endings had little to do with winter's grip and more to do with that face.

And then it came to her, the coalescence of a memory, the jigsaw of a half remembered dream coming back together again. Yes, of course.

The rat.

Four nights before, after tucking Lucette into bed with a headful of prayers—

("now I lay me down to sleep")

—there came the snap of the trap.

("I pray the Lord my soul to keep.")

Emily tiptoed into the kitchen, the floorboards of her ancient rental creaking underfoot, a sound that would have alerted the living to her presence on any other evening, although she suspected she was now dealing with the dead. The *almost* dead, as the stuttering florescent proved. The rat, which had been making meals out of their dry goods for the past two months, had been caught. Emily drew near, could smell the funk of dust and copper as the night thief kicked, once, twice. It studied her with a glare that seemed to say:

I don't understand what's happening. Not really. Yet here I am anyway.

I'm not ugly, not worthy of your fear. But you think I am.

Hungry. Hungry was all I ever was. Yet for this I was despised, gifted pain.

"Don't go in there," the woman said, her breath pluming in the frigid Chicago air.

Emily had no choice.

There was a job that needed to be done, and though the pay was a pittance, those pennies and dimes were enough to keep her landlord at bay and the heat on in the house. This was all the motivation she needed, ensuring the embers of her courage remained stoked. And they *needed* stoking. Always. Hunger was such sweet fuel, second only, perhaps, to gin. Though Emily had to admit it was a little early in the day for that, even for her.

Bones cracked as the old woman shook her head. "Don't." That ratty face twisted tighter. She stretched out her hands, fingers knotted like the roots of some weather-beaten tree. Searching for soil, for purpose.

I'm hungry to save you, the gesture implied.

Don't fear me.

I'm not the intruder here. You are.

And that place there, that place is the trap.

With the same finality, the same pity, which Emily lent the rat (a *thunk* to the head with one of her wooden spoons to finish what baited cheese and spring-loaded barbs had not), she continued up the steps. "I have to go."

"Then you're doomed."

"Yep, honey, I know that, too."

"No one who goes in that place comes out unscathed!"

Emily paused at the door, glanced back and realized the old woman was part of a larger group gathered at the corner, as they always were, whatever and wherever the facility. And of course, their constituents were always the same. Waifish soccer moms anchored to the ground by crucifixes. Preppy teenage boys whose prejudices had been adequately sculpted by the parents at their sides. Angry retirees who no longer felt safe wandering the highways in their RV's now that the infected weren't killed on sight. It was never any different, just the lost and the bored chanting the same things over and over again, like sad Christmas carolers, who in the heat of their hatred had forgotten what they were there to sing about.

Many of their hand-scrawled signs were incomprehensible, misspelled.

"LIFE IS 4 THE LIVING", "BRING OUT UR DED", "NO TOLERENCE 4 BONE EATERS", "LET'S FINISH THE JOB".

A shake of the head. Dug through her purse. Pulled out the keycard she'd been issued at the agency. Swiped the scanner.

Emily heard the *click* as the first of two glass doors slid open, revealing a security antechamber. A gasp of warm air ruffled her bangs as she steeled herself for the stink to come.

The lobby and unmanned reception were lost to shadows. Emily, determined to breathe through her mouth for a little longer, knew her nerves would emerge the victor here if she weren't careful. And that couldn't happen. Not now, not ever. Off-white walls adorned with paintings of sailboats and flowers seemed to absorb the light shining in through the glass doors at her back, as opposed to reflecting it. A row of uncomfortable looking plastic chairs on her left, a metal bin overflowing with magazines. Tinsel snaked about the place, shimmering in the dim. It was all so desperate.

Emily was alone.

The hallway stretched toward the back of the building, doors branching off to either side at regular intervals. At least it was brighter up ahead. She waited, shifting from foot to foot.

Distant clip-clopping shoes. Hissing electricity. An auto-tuned rendition of *Winter Wonderland*. The CD was scratched, the resulting melody unnerving her as though the singer's tongue, perverse and septic, were flickering in her ear.

She gripped her handbag, and inhaled through her nose for the first time.

There it was, the stink she knew so well—a heady mixture of piss, shit, and overcompensating bleach. But not all the bleach, not all the protesters in the world, could hide what was going on within these walls. And why, after all, should the truth be hidden? Emily had asked herself this question many times, though the answer always remained the same.

The ugliness of a truth doesn't make it a lie. Avoiding your responsibility does.

Emily started forward as a man emerged from a door halfway up the hall. In that very moment—as she gasped with shock and took one very definite step backwards—she detested herself.

He was a walking stick figure, skin sallow and covered in angry blemishes. His head was devoid of hair, and not just on his scalp either—there were no eyebrows or eyelashes to be found. His hands were twisted into arthritic claws, yellowed nails trimmed to the quick, which was standard procedure in hospices to keep the infected from scratching anyone. A line of drool swung from his lips, a pendulum reminding them all of his battle against the clock. Cloudy eyes, crusted with pus. A moan escaped him as he shambled closer. His gait was unsteady.

Get the fuck out of here, Sunshine, said a tiny voice in Emily's head. Its shrill tone was not unlike that of the ratty harbinger outside.

You're playing Russian roulette with your life every time you step into one of these damned places. So turn around and go.

Emily stood her ground. She could smell the man's decay.

Pump gas. Stack shelves. Jockey a cash register—Christ only knows the pay's better. Leave. The old bitch was right; nobody comes out of this place unscathed. Why do you do this to yourself? To Lucette?

Sunshine, you don't need to be here.

And with that her fear dissolved. The voice in her head often told lies, and none had been more prominent than that final manipulation. Because yes. Yes, she *did* need to be here.

A middle-aged woman followed the man out into the hallway and grabbed his arm just as he started to fall. Holding him up, allowing him to place his weight on her, the woman said, "Hey Speedy Gonzales, I told you to hold your horses. Lean on me."

When the woman noticed Emily standing there, she stopped. "Are you supposed to be in here?"

Unable to take her eyes off the ravaged man, Emily said, "I'm looking for Mrs. Woods. I'm sorry, there was no receptionist out front."

"Receptionist quit yesterday. What else is new? This place. *Pfft*. Woods' office is the last door on the left."

"Are you one of the nurses?"

"No, a relative. This is my husband. You a permanent newbie or just a temp?"

"Agency through and through, but if they want me, I'll stay."

"Ah! That's the attitude we want. Ain't that right, Speedy?"

The woman's husband did not reply.

Emily paused as she made to move past the couple. "It's nice to meet you. No doubt our paths will cross again." She saw the exaggerated length of the man's yellowed teeth, the beginning of his permanent smile, an awful irony considering his silent torture. "Is Speedy here—?"

"Yessum. Grade A. He's in FSU, the Final Stages Unit up there aways. They let me take him out every so often." Emily saw the way the woman's fingers gripped his arm. There would be bruising, no doubt. The man moaned. "We've been together almost twenty years. Now it's hard to tell how long he's got. But Speedy has his good days and his not so good days. Today's one of the latter. He's hardly said a word to me all morning. I'm not sure I know why I bother coming anymore."

A weight bloomed in Emily's chest, a sorrowful flower she had no choice but to cut off at the stem. Were she to let it live any longer, both Emily and that voice at the back of her head knew she wouldn't last longer than two minutes in this place. "Ma'am, is it a good idea for him to be out of bed?"

"Got to keep on moving. Ain't that right, Speedy? You tell the nice lady. After all, she'd keep on running if the devil was at her back, too." The woman locked eyes with Emily, her stare part plea, part spite. "They say if you keep them active, the blood pumping and all that, it can prolong—well, you know."

That's true, Emily thought to herself. *But look at him, honey. He's wasting away. He can hardly stand. Are you sure prolonging this is for the best?*

(The dead roam these halls.)

"I'm not ready to let go just yet." The woman's murmur was as delicate as fluttering moth wings. "But soon. Soon."

Then she got her husband moving and they hobbled back the way they had come. All that was left behind were the scents of death and cheap perfume, freckles of spit drying on the linoleum.

Emily, now flushed, took off her coat, draped it over her arm, and continued on. At the end of the corridor on her left, an open door revealed a black woman in blue scrubs sitting at a desk, typing furiously at a computer. She didn't seem to be aware that she was no longer alone until Emily rapped on the doorjamb.

Glancing Emily's way without pausing in her typing, the woman said, "Can I help you?"

"Mrs. Woods?"

"That's right."

"I'm Emily Samuels."

The clattering of keys stalled.

"Oh dear, is it that late already? I meant to meet you in the lobby."

"That's all right, I have my keycard already."

"Well, come in and have a seat. I have some paperwork for you to fill out and then I'll show you around the place, explain our procedures, introduce you to our guests."

"Guests?"

"We find it puts people more at ease than calling them patients."

"I see."

"Did the Right-to-Lifers out front give you grief?"

"Um, not much. A warning that I was doomed if I came in. The standard song and dance."

"A nuisance is what those folks are, harassing people on their way in and out like that. I called the police, but they said as long as none of the protestors came on the property there was nothing they could do. I suspect the authorities round here just don't give a toot."

"I have a thick skin," Emily said. "They can shout at me all they want, it won't bother me none."

Woods leaned her forearms on the desk. Cracked her neck. "Okay, girl. You a Ms. Samuels or you an Emily?"

"Emily, please."

"Emily. I read your file and saw that before you started up at the agency you were a nurse at Saint Michaels. Must've been making a good salary over there. I called your old supervisor. He raved about you, said how sorry they all were to see you go."

Woods paused as if she expected a response, but Emily wasn't sure what to say so she sat silently with her hands folded in her lap.

"I guess I just wondered why you'd give up that

kind of financial security at a state-of-the-art facility to come work for understaffed hospices like this dump, and for peanuts, no less. The Ministry has cut our budget; we never have enough hands on deck. Why choose this?"

Emily shrugged. "There's work here that needs to be done. Isn't that reason enough?"

"Hm. Where you from, Emily?"

"Nearby. The Russian quarter. I got a car if that's what this is about. I'm always on time."

"No, that's not what it's about. Not with an accent like yours. Where you from before you moved to The Windy City?"

"South Carolina."

"I thought as much."

"And that's supposed to mean what, exactly?"

"It's just that we've had trouble with people from down south coming into this place and bringing with them certain prejudices. Staff, I mean. My understanding is that they *still* don't treat the infected all that well down in South Carolina, regardless of the reform." Wood's eyed her, a feline flash that made Emily, a dog lover, dislike the woman even more. "I'm sure you can understand my concern. I'm the warden here. I need to look after everyone's wellbeing. Why the move to Chicago?"

Emily didn't spare a second with her reply. "I don't deal well with the heat."

And with that, the standoff cooled.

"Okay, Emily Samuels. Do well this week and we'll take you on permanent, assuming you want it. Monday to Friday. Six-thirty in the AM to three in the PM. There's no shortage of a shortage here, if you catch my drift."

"I'll sing for my supper given the chance. Your patients—*guests*—have largely been abandoned, but they are still human beings who deserve the best care. Especially at the end."

"Nice textbook answer, but have you ever actually been around the Grade A infected?"

Emily stiffened. "Yes. I've had extensive experience at the agency of working with C's, B's, and A's. The zombie contingent is—"

Woods threw up her hands. "No, no, no! We don't say 'zombie' here. Nor do we refer to our guests as 'smilers', or 'bone eaters' or whatever else it is you hear over there in the Russian quarter. It won't fly here, Emily. There's a reason those offensive B movies and trashy novels about the infected have been withdrawn from circulation, and banned. We, being a government funded non-profit, also don't want to promote—" cue finger quotation marks "—'negative perceptions'. Understood?"

"Crystalline."

Woods scrutinized her with a tilt of the head for a few moments before saying, "Okay, then let's get started. Welcome aboard."

The stink of the hospice followed her home.

Emily washed her hair three times, her scalp scratched and raw. The water was hotter than it should be. Steam cloyed, as strangulating as grief. There was no other option—she had to get out or faint. Emily sidestepped from the stall in her bathroom and toweled off. Finished, her hand rose to the mirror and carved a palm's width through the condensation.

I'm boiled. Boiled, but clean. That's all that matters.

It was nine in the evening and Emily wondered where the remainder of her afternoon had gone. It was only as she took inventory of her tired red-rimmed eyes that the weight of the day revealed itself. After leaving work, everything had become a series of events she'd walked through as though in a dream. The resulting fatigue was deep. It was in her bones, and the hot water in those pipes couldn't remedy that.

She remembered picking Lucette up from school, which was located two blocks away from their house. Convenient. This memory stuck because Emily had pulled up in her car with the awful fear that her daughter wouldn't be there waiting for her.

Due to the early starting time of her shift at the hospice, Emily had no choice but to let her ten-year-old take the bus from their shit-box, ground level apartment to Saint Mary's. Sure, she didn't have to walk far to catch a ride, the bus picking her up right outside, but that did little to curb the anxiety. Just crossing the empty lot between their front door and the stop could be a dangerous journey. Why? Because the world had claws. Complacency killed.

But Lucette had been waiting there for her, of course, backpack dangling from one shoulder, a smile from ear to ear. She was so tiny in her bulky snow jacket. Emily's relief had been instantaneous. Yes, this arrangement *might* just work.

Her daughter had leapt into the car and told her about her day, only parts of which Emily could recall now. Something about a new substitute teacher, a man who had spent time in Japan and was teaching them how to make origami cranes. Lucette had been beaming over this, a surprise.

Oh—origami, then. Not what I'd anticipated as your newest phase, but okay.

Lucette was a lot of things, gregarious and easy to anger, not the kind of girl who would find the folding of paper fun. Generally speaking.

Well, what do I know? It's so hard keeping up with it all.

Time ticked by on autopilot.

They then went to the grocery store, where Lucette pushed the trolley, as she loved to do. Before Emily knew it, they were back home, cooking up a pot of spaghetti, the news playing in the background, the reporter saying something about a bone eater that had been wandering around the city dockyards and killed a tourist. Dishes washed, packed away. A boiled kettle. A teabag bled in the mug. Warmth. And finally, all that scouring in the shower.

The mirror fogged over. Emily turned away and sat down on the bathroom stool, her knees cracking. Had a truck hit her at some point? It felt as though one had.

Tomorrow will be easier. The next day always is.

She wrapped herself in a nightgown and walked into the hall.

Lucette was lying on her stomach in front of the television, head propped in her hands, feet in the air. "Okay, darlin'," Emily said. "Time for bed."

"Five more minutes?"

"Nope. Big day tomorrow. For both of us."

Her daughter relented after the usual push and pull, and switched off the set. Lucette was getting taller by the day and beautiful in a tom-boyish way, despite the pig-tails and legs made for dancing. Emily smiled. She'd never thought it possible to love someone so much.

Lucette slinked into her arms, smelling of soap and bubblegum. "What's the matter, Mom? You seem sad."

"Just exhausted, darlin'."

"Is your new work good?"

"Doing a good thing rarely feels good. I'll earn my sleep, let's put it that way." Emily planted a kiss on the crown of her head. "I'll be fine."

"Will you tuck me in?"

"Of course."

After prayers, and after promises to not let the bedbugs bite, Emily left Lucette in the dark. There had been a time when there had to be a nightlight in the room at all times, but things had changed somewhere along the line. Unlike her mother, Lucette seemed to be growing braver by the day. Emily was almost envious, and mourned the steel of her own resolve. Sure, she presented as hard-nosed to others—and damn it, she *had* to be at times—but by night, as she tiptoed through the house and extinguished every bulb, she knew better.

Emily's room was tidy. Tomorrow's uniform slung over the back of a chair. Sneakers on a piece of newspaper. A place for everything and everything in its place—except for one thing. There was a new baseball bat on the bed. Emily had bought it yesterday for twenty-nine dollars. Lucette would love it, she being the kind of girl who didn't care much for dolls—not anymore, not since the Raggedy Ann she'd nicknamed Natalia. The Dodgers, on the other hand, were legendary. And her daughter had quite a swing on her, too. This made Emily proud.

WHERE THE DEAD GO TO DIE

Maybe I should get her a book on origami for Christmas as well, considering how psyched she was about it today. After my first paycheck.

Earthquakes, the weather, a ten-year-old's whim—none of these could be predicted, not really. No matter what people said. There were always variables, and those variables kept Emily on her toes. Not necessarily a bad thing.

She was convinced the bat would be a sure-fire hit on Christmas day in two weeks' time. Tomorrow after her shift, she would pick up some wrapping paper from the corner store, something with reindeer on it or little Santa Clauses. It would be gift *numero uno* under this year's tree—an artificial cheapie with bent branches. Mother and daughter had erected it the prior weekend.

Her fingers curled around the bat. Gripping it made her long for summer. She hid it in her walk-in wardrobe and eased the door shut. A little groan of exhaustion escaped her. The mattress called and she had every intention of answering.

Emily thumped down and the bedsprings sang their lullaby. Silence.

The streetlight outside her window lent just enough peace of mind. Emily studied it now, watched all those snowflakes falling in straight lines like a rain of dead things. There was no wind. No stars.

Reality dissolved at some point. In her dream she stood at the windowsill, hands flush against the glass. She looked out at the empty lot next door. The ground should have been flat as dead calm water with all that virgin downfall. No. There were corpses upon corpses there; frozen hands pitched this way and that. Their smiles wide enough for all of Chicago's rats to make homes from their mouths.

INTERLUDE ONE

Take a square piece of paper. Fold the top corner to the bottom. Crease, open again, and then fold the paper in half, sideways this time. Turn the square over, crease diagonally, open, and then fold in the opposite direction.

HIS VOICE LIKE honey, as it always was. "Did you grab the card, babe?"

SMOKE BREAK WITH MAMA METCALF

EMILY MET MAMA Metcalf her third day on the job.

Three hours in and overdue for her first break, Emily sought refuge in the courtyard accessible through the break room. Although 'courtyard' seemed too fancy a description for the space, which she could tell from peering through the staffroom window was empty except for a weathered picnic table and the woman sitting at it. Emily gripped her fourth coffee of the morning in one hand and gripped the handle with the other.

She closed her eyes and in the dark imagined warmer weather greeting her. Sunshine on her face. The smell of wafting barbeque. Yes, the outdoor setting might even pass as halfway inviting mid-year, so long as she ignored the enclosing nine-foot wall, the one fringed with bales of razor-wire.

Ignored the dead pigeon snagged in the barbs.

The door creaked open. As expected, the day was bitter, but Emily found the frigid air preferable to the antiseptic foulness she was leaving behind, if only for fifteen minutes. Potential pneumonia was preferable to staying a single unpaid minute inside the hospice.

The past three days had been a blur of soiled sheets, vomit clean-up duties, sponge baths, assisted feeds—work normally performed by the unpaid volunteers. She suspected Woods was testing the elasticity of her dedication, giving her all the shit chores to see if she would stick with it.

Woods doesn't know anything about me if she thinks I'll be scared off that easy.

Emily pulled her coat tight around her. Though it wasn't currently snowing, a fresh layer of white covered the ground. Her footsteps crunched as she crossed the courtyard.

The woman at the picnic table was short, had brown hair streaked with gray, and wore a white set of scrubs. Her back was to the building, the vapor of her breath drifting up like smoke signals. If she heard Emily's approach, she didn't react.

"Hello there," Emily said when she was close enough to reach out and touch the woman's shoulder. She turned around; her creased face lit up in a smile.

The woman had to be in her 70s, at least. Emily also noted that it hadn't been the woman's breath she'd seen before; rather smoke from the crudely rolled cigarette pinched tight between her lips. "Oh, hey sugar. You must be new here."

"Yes, I started earlier this week," Emily said, walking around to sit on the opposite side of the picnic table. "I'm Emily Samuels. I don't think we've met."

"I've been out with a stomach bug, this is my first day back in a couple weeks. You don't want to bring sickness in this place, sugar. It'll only end up killing these folks quicker, and that'll just leave us with even *more* work to do. Name's Brenda Metcalf, but you can call me Mama Metcalf. Everybody does."

"Nice to meet you." And Emily sincerely meant that. There was something about the woman's presence that made her feel at ease.

Is there a trace of a southern lilt to her accent? Yes, I think there just might be.

Sounds like the home place.

"I roll my own," Mama Metcalf said when she noticed Emily eyeing the cigarette. "It's cheaper to buy the loose tobacco and papers than getting a carton these days."

"I see. So this is the smoking area?"

"Not really. Ain't supposed to be no smoking anywhere on the property, but Woods looks the other way so long as I don't leave my butts lying around. I put 'em in a sandwich baggie and take 'em with me when I leave. You want one?"

Emily shook her head. "I used to, but my husband made me quit when I got pregnant with our daughter."

"Yeah, my oldest son's always after me to shake the habit, so I tell him it's my only real pleasure in life. Besides, I don't usually finish a cigarette, just take a few puff-puffs."

Emily sipped her coffee and wondered what life must be like for all the old women of the world whose sole pleasures came in the form of cheap hand-rolled cigarettes. But then her mind turned to the bottle of gin she had stashed away in her rental and decided she was in no position to judge.

"You're not wearing a wedding ring," Mama Metcalf said.

Emily thought of herself as a person divided into three parts. There was the Old Emily, the part that had quite happily existed up to the day she forgot the card. Then there was the part of her that would have suffered through Mama Metcalf's question, a question that would have made her hands draw onto her lap, tucked away and hidden, curled up like wounded animals ashamed of their scars. Not anymore. She was Emily the Third—a mother who would never allow herself the disgrace of ever missing a beat.

"I'm not married anymore."

"I hear ya. Finally divorced my old man about five years back. Straw that broke the camel's hump was when he beat me with the Christmas tree."

Emily was so stunned by the comment that she didn't know how to respond. She was still trying to think of something to say when the door to the building opened and the male nurse she was working with earlier popped his head out. "Hey, New Girl."

Emily stiffened, her lips stretching into a rictus of a smile. "Just a reminder my name's Emily, not 'New Girl'. All good?"

"No need to get your panties in a bunch, honey. It's a revolving door of nurses around here, so I don't bother learning names 'til I'm sure they're gonna stick around."

A sharp retort rose to her lips. Swallowed it down. She'd only just met Mykel ("Pronounced like Michael but spelled M-Y-K-E-L," he said when they first met, though Emily doubted that was the spelling on his birth certificate) and her tolerance for him was already waning. Emily hoped they wouldn't have to work together too often, but considering how short-staffed the hospice was, she had a feeling she was fresh out of luck.

"I gotta get back inside, almost time to give out meds," Mama Metcalf said, stubbing her cigarette on the heel of her shoe, and then placing it inside a Ziploc bag. She sealed it up and stuffed it in a small black purse on the bench next to her. "Also wanna see what they got good in the vending machine. I forgot to pack a lunch today."

"Well, it's not much," Emily said, "but I brought a couple of bananas from home and left them on top of the staff fridge inside. You're welcome to them."

"Thank you but I can't eat bananas no more," Mama Metcalf said, scuttling back across the courtyard. "I had my gallbladder took out a couple years ago, so I can't filter the seeds."

With that quizzical statement, she walked through the door Mykel was holding open for her and disappeared.

"She's a hoot, but I'm confused," Emily said.

Mykel walked over to the picnic table. "Confused by which part? The part where she thinks those little black things in a banana are real seeds, or the part where she thinks the gallbladder's job is to *filter* seeds?"

"Both actually. She's a nurse?"

"Oh no, Mama Metcalf is one of our non-medical volunteers."

"But she just said she was going to be giving out meds."

"Yeah, well, truth is this place is barely scraping by with what little funding we get, and private donations are one step up from zilch. Rules get bent."

"Great, so I'm using my BSN degree to clean shitty sheets while some senior citizen off the street is giving meds."

"You're just going through your initiation period, but you must be moving up in the world, New Girl. Woods wants you in her office pronto to observe an intake interview."

Emily stood. "Intake? I didn't know we were expecting any new guests today."

"We weren't. We had a drop and run this morning. A kid. Looks like we're going to be cramming a new zombie on the hall."

Emily frowned at Mykel as she passed. "It's against facility policy to call them 'zombies'. You know that, right?"

"New Girl," Mykel said as he followed her into the building, "you're not going to last here very long if you don't lighten up."

INTAKE

AFTER STOWING HER coat in the break room, Emily found Woods outside the door to her office, holding a bottle of Yoo-hoo chocolate in her hands. At first glance, her supervisor's face was stoic. A second pass proved otherwise.

Emily detected shards of unease in Woods' expression, the pointy ends driving in, causing noticeable pain. And she wasn't doing a good job of hiding it, either. Emily almost asked if she was okay, but snatched the words from the tip of her tongue and tucked them away as though she'd been caught red-handed with something humiliating.

What an awful revelation. Discovering someone you're obliged to respect is human.

No matter how passive the mask someone wore, emotions lurked beneath the surface.

In some alternate reality, Emily suspected robots must be the ones delivering this line of work. Machines programmed to express dignity and empathy on cue, deflecting care's heartbreak. Maybe the hospice workers of the future were coin-operated things, little profit contrivances—boy-oh-boy would the taxpayers of America love that. These corridors would ring with

SERVICE REQUIRED alerts, a symphony of turning cogs, whilst beneath it all, beneath that surface, weeping went unheard. But this wasn't the future. This wasn't science fiction. They were only human after all—tender beings in slipping masks.

"Emily, I wanted to have a word with you before we go in."

The door to Woods' office was closed, but Emily could see a head capped with curly black hair through the window. "Mykel said it was a kid."

"I'm afraid he's right."

"How old?"

"Twelve."

"Oh, Jesus." How could she *not* think of Lucette, who was only two years younger? *There but for the grace of God*, assuming He, or She, existed.

Emily had her doubts, as she figured any sane person would in this unforgiving world. Sure, she insisted her daughter recite prayers before bed, but it was impossible to tell if anyone was listening. Emily's Catholicism had been drilled into her by her parents, two big-boned Southerners who took their religion 'straight up' right until the end when God repaid their devotion with a set of His and Her's matching heart attacks. However, from an early age Emily harbored doubts. The Bible stories they told at Mass just didn't make sense. How could two of every animal in the world fit on one boat, and where did they all go to the bathroom? How could someone be their own father, or their own son? Why would Jesus have to let himself be killed in order to forgive all people of their sins, couldn't he just say "You're forgiven" and be done with it? Why was Adam and Eve's desire for knowledge something to be punished? And the standard answer she received when she posed these questions to her parents, "You just have to have faith", seemed a convenient way of not having to give an answer. Once her parents were gone, she'd stopped going to church altogether, part of her belief sealed in those caskets. Despite this, Emily found herself passing on some of the traditions to her daughter and scouring the sky for answers among the satellites and shooting stars. Religion was a drug after all, one she hadn't realized she was dependent on until she was almost free of it.

That didn't mean she had to respect the dealer, though.

So Lucette carried the torch for the two of them. And if her ten-year-old reached an age when she either owned this belief or cast it aside, well, Emily would be the happy beneficiary of that judgment. She trusted her daughter *that* much.

Woods lowered her voice. "The boy's understandably upset. He's been crying since he got here."

"Did his parents really drop him at the curb?"

"They brought him into the lobby and signed him in. They didn't stick around."

"I just don't—how? I would never let my daughter go through something like this alone."

"They're scared. Even today, there's a plethora of misinformation out there about infection."

"Then you educate yourself. You don't do *this*," Emily said, perhaps a little too vehement. "He's not trash."

"That's enough, Ms. Samuels." Woods' clipped tone cut through her escalating anger like a slap to the face.

"I'm sorry. I can't get my head round folks abandoning their kids like that."

"Our concern is for the child, not his parents. Look, I need you to pull yourself into line. I can't have you in that room with me if you're going to get emotional. What that boy needs right now is a calming, stabilizing influence. Understood?"

Emily took a deep breath, steadied herself. Nodded.

Woods scrutinized her. "I'm giving you a chance. You're here to observe. Let me do all the talking. If I sense an outburst a-comin' I'll send you out of the room and out of a job. Do we understand each other?"

"Crystalline."

"Good. The boy's name is Robert Hopkins. The dignity we offer here begins with calling people by their preferred name. He's a Robby. That's your first lesson."

"Got it."

Woods opened the door and stepped into her office, Emily following along behind. "Here you go, Robby," Woods said, holding the drink out to the boy.

He—

(Lucette)

—turned to face them. Coldness reached into Emily's chest and clenched tight. No, it wasn't her daughter. It had been little more than a momentary lapse, a slip of the mask.

She cleared her throat, and stoked heat to melt the ice inside.

There was innocence and beauty in the boy's eyes. Stray tears clung to his cheeks, but the ferocity of the storm had abated. He sniffled twice, wiped his nose with a sleeve, and took the drink, mumbling gratitude.

He was skeletal; skin five shades whiter than it should be. He looked as though he hadn't slept in weeks, which, Emily guessed, was likely the case. With infection came fevers and nightmares people referred to as 'the screamers'—terrible glimpses into the Hell that had claimed them. Or so they said. These dreams lingered with the infected throughout the incubation period, though there came a point when the screaming stopped. For family members, this silence was considered one of the most difficult parts of the changing. Their loved ones no longer considered the nightmares unwelcome.

Acquiescence to their fate.

Woods sat behind her desk and indicated that Emily should have a seat in the plastic chair; it was positioned against the far wall, which was covered in children's drawings.

Ha, so I guess there's a maternal bone in your body after all, Woods, she thought. *Somewhere.*

"Robby, this is Emily. She'll be sitting in with us. Is that okay?"

He glanced at her, shrugged and nodded at the same time.

"Thank you, Robby. I like your sweater," Emily said, searching for common ground.

"Thanks," he replied, toying with the Tyrannosaur's skull woven into the wool. "I want to be a paleontologist when I grow up."

It was time to change the subject, and quick.

Woods opened a folder and plucked a pen out of a Mason jar crammed with writing utensils. She clicked the ballpoint and sat poised with pen over the paper. "I'm going to ask you a series of questions now, Robby. If you don't understand anything, you let me know, and I'll try to make it clearer. Don't be afraid to admit if you don't know all the answers. If you need to take a break at any time—"

"I'm good," the boy said, opening the Yoo-hoo and downing half of it in one swallow. The infected craved sugar. Fats. And with time, marrow. "I'm sorry I cried."

Despite being told to let Woods do all the talking, Emily leaned forward and said, "There's no shame in that, Robby. We all have to let it out, don't we Ms. Woods?"

"That's right."

Robby leveled a piercing stare at Emily. "I'll be okay. I'm not a baby."

Emily was taken aback by the tone of the boy's voice—so firm and sure and *adult*. Then again, she had to remind himself that twelve was almost a teenager, and a teenager was almost a man. She found the notion disturbing in a way she didn't understand at first, until she realized she was thinking of Lucette again, about how she wasn't really a kid anymore, and before long she would be going out into the world on her own where Emily wouldn't be able to protect her.

"Robby," Woods said, "can you tell me how you acquired the infection?"

"Got bit."

The scratching of the pen on the form. "One bite or multiple?"

"One was all it took."

"And where is it located?"

"On my ankle."

Emily glanced down at the boy's feet and saw the print on his socks below the cuffs of his jeans. Batman insignias. She suppressed a sigh. Robby could have idolized Superman, Thor, or any one of a million heroes with strength to spare and imperviousness to bullets and bites. Only he'd settled on a mere mortal in crusader's pajamas instead.

And mortals, as they all knew, could die. A self-fulfilling prophecy.

More scratching from the pen. "How did it happen?" Woods asked.

"I was somewhere I wasn't supposed to be," he replied.

Emily understood that comment for what it was, not a conclusion Robby had drawn for himself, but something he'd been *told*. As a parent, Emily recognized its desperate condescension a little too well.

"My folks let me go to a Halloween festival with some friends, but all the rides were for kids and the haunted house was a joke. Just guys in sheets and dummies rigged to jump out at you. Beyond lame. I tried to talk a couple of my friends into climbing the security fence to explore the woods behind the fairgrounds. They didn't want to, they were scared. To be honest, so was I, only I wanted to prove something, you know? That I was brave, or something. They call me sissy at school."

Something Robby said raised a red flag for Emily and, glancing at Woods, she could see that the other woman realized it too. Neither of them spoke, waiting for Robby to finish his story.

"I went deeper into the woods. It was like I was on

a dare, like I was daring myself. It was dark, but I had a flashlight app on my phone and I was using it to see where I was going. I was just starting to think I should turn back when I heard a noise up ahead, a kind of moaning. I followed it to a ravine. The light from my phone didn't reach that far, but I could just make out a figure down there, and it looked like it was pinned by a tree that'd fallen over. I shouldn't have gone further. I know that. I thought it was someone hurt. You believe me, don't you?"

"Of course we do," Emily said.

"I figured I'd go help and maybe end up a hero, get my picture on all the news websites and everything. I called out, only whoever was down there didn't answer. Well, I wasn't a complete idiot; I decided I'd climb down about halfway so I could get a better look. Only I slipped and fell. Landed right next to him. He wasn't pinned down after all. I know it sounds stupid, but I remember picking up my phone, which was on the ground next to me, and looking at the screen. It was cracked. I thought to myself, 'Shit—Mom's gonna have my guts for garters over that.' *Ha!*

"I turned the light on him. He hadn't fully turned yet, but I reckon he was close. He hardly had any hair left. His skin was white. Had the smile—that's the worst. He was homeless, I guess. He was snappin' his teeth and clawin' at me. I screamed like a girl and tried to crawl back up the ravine, only I kept sliding back down. You know those dreams when you're trying to get away from something bad, and everything's in slow-motion and the ground goes all quicksandy on you? It was just like that.

"I thought I was okay. Only I wasn't." Robby cast

his eyes downward. "The whole way home it didn't really *click* what happened. I was too worried about my cracked phone. So stupid." He looked up at them again. "You believe me, right?"

Emily and Woods exchanged a glance and with a lift of her chin, Woods gave Emily permission to ask the question that was on both their minds.

"Yes, Robby. But I just want to check one thing. You said this happened the night of the Halloween festival?"

The boy nodded.

The pen froze, no scratching, and Woods said, "So you're saying you were bitten almost two months ago?"

Another silent nod.

Woods seemed at a loss for words, which Emily figured happened about as often as an honest politician got elected to public office—and yet they still did, each bringing with them additional infection-specific prohibition. To her credit, she recovered her composure. "I checked the Ministry's infected registry website and didn't see your name on it."

"No, I don't guess you did. You'll put it up there now, right?"

"Yes, but that should've already happened. Everyone exposed to the infection is required to report their status within 48 hours so their names can be added. Since you're a minor, it would have been your parents' responsibility. Were they aware of this?"

Robby stared back at his interviewers. His eyes welled again.

"You hid it from them," Emily said. A statement, not a question.

The silent nod that was becoming a trademark.

"When did they find out?" Woods asked.

"A week ago. I know it was wrong, that I should've told them right away, but I was scared. They thought I was sick or something, even wanted to take me to a doctor. Dad's got the diabetes and they thought it might be that. They had me in a corner! I—I spilled my guts. They just glared at me, like they'd been told I was dead. I was wearing my dad's old cap at the time. I dunno. I always loved it. It's his from when he was a kid and lived in Maine. It's got the words I'VE GOT MOXIE written across the front, you know, like the drink. When I told them about being attacked, Dad didn't saying nothin', he just crossed the room and ripped the hat right off my head. I wish he'd yelled at me instead, or hit me. You don't know my folks, they hate bone eaters."

Woods opened her mouth as if she were going to correct the boy's use of the derogatory term, but thought better of it and kept her silence.

"You a bone eater, you're as good as dead to them. They had a friend, I seen her in their old wedding photos, she got bit. They cut her out of their lives. Just like that. You've probably seen them outside this building holding signs and yelling nasty things at everybody that walked by. I even heard my father say once that he wished the Ministry would go back to getting rid of zombies like they did in the old days."

Emily stiffened, cleared her throat. "But you're their child."

Robby looked at her, and while his eyes were still innocent and beautiful, they were also tainted with motes of cynicism. Betrayal. "I had a broken toy once. It didn't work. We took it back to the shop and Dad threw it on the counter. 'It's defective,' is what he said to the girl standing there. And that's how I feel, too. They couldn't get rid of me fast enough.

"I snuck out of bed last night and listened at their bedroom door. Mom was crying the whole time, I think she at least feels bad about it, but Dad said that as far as he's concerned he no longer has a son. He hasn't looked at me or talked directly to me since I told them."

"I'm sorry," Woods said, and Emily wasn't surprised when the woman said no more. She wasn't one to sugarcoat, a trait that some found abrasive, but which Emily was growing to admire.

Robby shrugged. "Like I said. *Defective.*"

Emily felt hairline cracks forming in her composure. The boy in the dinosaur sweater was displaying bravery and strength no kid his age should rightly have to. He had Moxie, all right. Moxie by the bucket load. But that didn't change the fact that Robby Hopkins was of an age when his concerns should've been revolving around getting to the next level of some silly video game, or figuring out how to patch a busted bike tire, or maybe even facing the challenges of Japanese origami head on. And behind him all the way, there should be watchful parents who loved without condition, even in the worst circumstances.

Especially in the worst circumstances.

"Now I need you to really concentrate and be truthful," Woods continued. "Can you think of anyone that you may have exposed? Maybe you got cut and your mother cleaned it up, anything like that?"

Shaking his head emphatically, Robby said, "No, I was careful."

"You're sure?"

"I'm positive. I don't want anyone else going through this."

Woods began scribbling notes on the new form. Emily wanted to say something to the boy, offer some words of solace, a panacea for his pain, but none seemed adequate to the task.

"Of course, we'll have to alert the authorities about the resurrected individual that bit you," Woods said. "That's a potential danger to others that has to be dealt with."

"I tried to deal with it myself," Robby said quietly. "I went back a week later with a baseball bat. Only the man was gone."

Woods kept her gaze steady. "I see." She opened a file drawer in her desk and rummaged around for a moment, coming up with another form. "In light of this new knowledge regarding how long you've been infected, I have a few additional questions to ask you. Do you know how the infection is spread? During the incubation period it's through bites, body fluids, transfusions, sharing needles. After turning, bites alone."

"Yes. They teach us that in school." The boy sat upright and thumped his fists against his knees. "I'm not an idiot. And I thought you said you believed me!"

Woods spared a glance at Emily, who could feel another crack forming. She fought against it. "That's not what this is about, Robby. It's important we get all our facts straight. I know this is hard, but once it's done, it's done. We're going to take wonderful care of you here."

"Robby," Woods began, "it's important we see the bite wound. Can you show it to us?"

"No. I don't want to."

"In order to secure the government funding required to help you, we need to provide documentation to the board, a photograph of the contact-to-contact area."

"I said no."

Woods leaned back. "I'm so sorry, Robby. You don't have a choice on the matter."

The twelve-year-old glared back at his two interviewers. In requesting to see the wound, Emily could plainly see that they were at risk of re-opening it.

Emily and Woods jolted in their chairs, the legs screeching against the linoleum, as Robby leapt to his feet. The two women stood, calling to the boy to stop. He threw the door open, conjuring a draft that sent the children's drawings on the walls into a flap like a pin board of not-quite-dead butterflies.

"Fuck you both!" he yelled, scuttling from sight.

Emily stepped into the hallway and saw Robby at the glass entrance/exit security door, which required either a swipe pass or a five-digit override code to open. His thin silhouette stood against the glare of the transparent barricade, as he tried to pry the sliding glass apart with his hands. When he realized this was getting him nowhere fast, he resorted to beating. The sound thundered through the corridor, drawing attention. Heads jack-in-a-boxed from their rooms to see what all the commotion was.

"Don't do that, Robby," Emily said, heart racing. Close. "It's no help."

Woods flanked her side, a cell phone in hand. "Layton," she whispered into the receiver. "Meet me in corridor 1. Code T-4 underway. Be delicate." She hung up.

Defeated and weak, Robby backed against the wall, slid to the floor. He buried his head in his hands.

"Can we have some privacy here, thank you?" Woods called to those lingering up the hallway. Those rubberneckers, staff and guests alike, withdrew into their rooms.

Emily crouched in front of their new intake, the chameleon who was by turns adult and then infantile. It was an alarming balancing act to witness, like watching someone dancing for their life on the head of a pin.

"Ms. Samuels," Woods said, "let the boy be. Security's on the way."

Emily raised a hand to her supervisor. "It's okay. Isn't it, Robby?"

She faced the boy once more, shimmied over to join him. "I'm just going to plant myself right here. That fine by you?"

Robby nodded.

Now that she was close enough, Emily noted the musky smell of mold and dried sweat on the boy's dinosaur sweater. Heat radiated from his skin in waves.

"I'm here with you," she said. Soft. Words just for him, a gift he appeared to be responding to.

"This whole thing sucks so bad," he said between sobs. "I'm not crying. I'm not."

"I know. You're a brave young man."

Robby snorted, wiped his eyes. "But I *am* scared."

"Are you kidding? Me too. I'm terrified all the time. For my daughter, for me. Terrified of this place." In a very hushed tone. "Terrified of *her*," Emily said, tilting her head in Woods' direction.

Robby caved, even managed half a giggle. "Really?"

"Oh, laws yeah." Emily gave him a small shove with her shoulder. He pushed back. "You're not alone here, Robby. Nobody's perfect. We're all, well, we're all sick in different ways. We're all defective."

"I—I guess so."

"Well, I *know* so."

They watched Layton, the facilities' mid-week security guard, come clip-clopping down the corridor. His girth was considerable, which only made the baton clipped to his belt appear novelty sized. He wheezed for breath at Woods' side, awaiting instruction. Just as Emily had done to her, she raised her hand to him. "Wait a moment."

Robby locked eyes with Emily for the first time since bursting out of the office. "I'm sorry I swore."

"It's okay. I've dropped more than my share of F-bombs. You didn't do anything wrong."

"Yeah, I did. I lied in there."

"I know. I've got a daughter 'bout your age. I can tell white fibs a mile off."

"It's not white, though. It's black. Black through and through."

"You can tell me, Robby. I know some things are hard to say out loud, trust me. Speakin' a truth, though, it's healing sometimes."

Robby faced the door again, touched the glass paneling with a shaking hand. When he dropped his arm there was a perfectly formed sweat print left behind. It faded, swallowed up and devoured by the merciless hospice chill.

Emily and Robby watched Woods and Layton exchanging gestures. After a beat of misinterpreted body language, the routine wrapped up and they both about-turned and headed toward her office. The door creaked shut and clicked into place.

"It's just you and me now, Robby," Emily said. "You and me versus the world."

"Thank you."

In her desperation to offer additional comfort—to really let him know how much she cared, and she *did*—Emily made a decision. She took her right hand and placed it on his left knee, a simple, measured act of consolation. The moment her fingers lit on his jeans the boy jerked away. It was as though Emily's touch were nothing less than electric.

And with that, she knew.

Be they white or black, the veils of his lie were now drawn back for her to see. That he didn't get up and run again was, in some ways, a privilege—testament to this fragile chameleon's trust in her. Or maybe it was simply that the truth was too exhausting. Either way, he was here and so was she, but wedged between them was honesty, ugly and pure. They were never going to find a bite mark because the child hadn't been bitten. He'd been raped.

Again, that default line danced through her head: *There but for the grace of God.*

"Oh, Robby."

"Tell me something," he said. Firm. He understood that she understood. "Be straight with me."

"Anything," Emily replied. "Anything at all."

Robby glared at her. Those motes of cynicism and betrayal in his eyes that she'd noted earlier coalesced into tears and dripped down his cheeks, flawless diamonds of hurt. "The infection, I've heard it usually takes a year before it kills you and *turns* you. Is that right?"

Emily took a moment before answering. "It's 8 to 15 months for the infection to run its course, typically. The longest anyone has ever survived with the infection is 3 and a half years, but there are people on record who've died from it in as quickly as 3 months."

"And it always kills you, right?"

"Yeah, honey. There's no cure."

The boy inhaled, let out a shaky breath. "I hear it's painful."

"Here at the hospice, we'll keep you as comfortable as possible, that I promise you."

"And when the time comes, when I die and come back—"

(a mosaic of red splatters on a bright blue mailbox)

"—someone will put me down?"

(a scream cut short)

Emily blinked. She was hollow. "It's not like that. Our guests can choose to have a loved one present if they desire."

"Guest? I'm not a guest here. Will you promise never to call me that?"

Yes. Yes, she believed she could do that for the boy who was always a Robby and never a Robert, and gladly told him so. Beneath all the diplomacy and corporate lingo, he was right.

Guests could leave anytime they wished.

A shadow fell over them. They looked up. Emily beamed. "Robby," she began, "this is Mama Metcalf.

She's my friend and she'll be your friend too if you like."

"Hello, Robby," came that familiar dulcet voice.

"Mama Metcalf is a volunteer here. She'll show you to your room. Would that be okay?"

"I guess so."

"Come on, young'un," Mama Metcalf said, holding out her hand. "Between you and me, yours is the nicest room in the place."

A brief smile flicked the corners of Robby's lips, and he took Mama Metcalf's hand and allowed her to help him up. They walked the corridor together, rounded the corner, Robby sparing a quick look back in Emily's direction before vanishing.

Emily felt further cracks on cracks. The walls encroached in on her.

"Christ almighty—"

The door to Woods' office opened and the stern-faced supervisor stepped out, with their security guard following soon after. Layton waddled away, his unused baton still sheathed by his side—as useless as Lancelot without a stone to strike.

Woods waited until they were alone before turning to Emily and saying, "You did well."

"I feel absolutely empty."

"I know. It's never easy. Kids are the worst."

"Robby was raped."

Woods closed her eyes. "I suspected that might be the case. It's—it's not the first time I've come across this. But we still have a job to do."

"What's going to happen when we report that Robby was infected two months ago and kept it a secret?"

"We're not reporting it," Woods said firmly. "As far as we're concerned, he only just acquired the infection."

"But we're required by law—"

"I know what the laws are, Ms. Samuels, but I also know that the current administration's tolerance for infected individuals is as thin as chiffon lace. If we report this, it will open a whole can of worms that'll cause a lot of problems. The Ministry will want to show they aren't soft on infected issues, and they'll see this as an opportunity to make an example of this situation. They won't care how he contracted the infection."

Emily folded her arms across her chest. "Well, maybe his parents should be made an example of."

"Only his parents wouldn't be the example. They aren't the ones that hid the infection."

"You don't mean—he's just a *kid,* a kid who has been through some serious trauma."

"If you're so sure that would matter to them, then by all means, make the call."

Emily said nothing, her shoulders sagging in defeat. Woods was right. Those people standing outside protesting—a group that Robby's own parents sometimes belonged to—wouldn't even view him as a person anymore.

"Okay," Woods said, "Take twenty minutes to decompress. By then, Robby should be settled. I want you to record his vitals, talk with him a bit. Get written consent to make a referral to a social worker and a doctor. Considering how he contracted the infection he'll need both."

Emily shuddered.

Robby must have been terrified down there in that

dark ravine, the jingle-jangle of the Halloween fair obscuring his pleas for help. And yes, as brave as he could be, there must have been screams. Emily could only hope it hadn't lasted long. That the boy hadn't also been bitten was a marvel in and of itself. She could almost see the smiler when she blinked, the soiled clothes torn and ill fitting, its white rictus getting closer in staccato leaps.

Dead leaves crunching. A scramble. All that desperation, the hunger. And then afterwards, Robby's long and lonely walk home, the Moxie cap no doubt askew, as his friends continued to play, satisfied with artificial scares and candy-sick stomachs.

"And don't forget to put all of this in your notes," Woods said, snapping Emily from one ugly reality back to another.

"Yes. Yes, of course."

Woods gave her a polite 'now-on-your-way' nod and made for the door to her office. Her fingers hovered over the handle. "You have a way with kids, Ms. Samuels," she said over her shoulder. "I'm sure you're a fine mother."

"Thank you." Emily made to leave, paused. "Can I ask you something?"

"Shoot." Woods turned around.

"All those forms are on the computer, why were you filling them out by hand?"

"Just a psychological thing. People view the computer as something cold and impersonal. But pen and paper, that's something more intimate. Even if people aren't aware of it on a conscious level, it puts them more at ease, makes them feel they're being listened to."

Emily tilted her head in response, thinking there was a lot she could learn from this woman, and in turn, hoped that lesson went both ways.

INTERLUDE TWO

Using the creases you have made, bring the top three corners of the paper to the bottom. Flatten. After this, fold the top triangular wings into the center and unfold. Finish this set by folding the top of the square downward, and crease. Unfold.

"**DID YOU GRAB** the card, babe?" Jordan asked.

The look Emily gave her husband said it all: Why of course she'd forgotten to grab the card. It was inside on the study desk where she'd stopped to write the inscription, thinking, *So do I make this out to Kevin or his parents? It's not like a three-year-old is going to read it anyway. He'll just throw it aside as he rips off the wrapping.* Emily couldn't blame him for that. Lucette, who was the same age, had done a similar thing at her birthday party the month before. And although they often pretended otherwise, adults weren't so different—everyone knew cards were an overpriced pit stop on the road to the good stuff. But formalities were important.

They help trick us into thinking things are normal again.

Emily ended up making the card out to both Kevin and his parents, Conrad and Sally, old college friends of Jordan's. They had lost touch for a while there, a gap that having kids bridged. There were over 60 daycares in Charleston, so it was a little surprising to run into two familiar faces at their first parents/teachers 'meet-and-greet' day. The world, as they said, was small.

A little too small for Emily's liking, especially in the south, where even the biggest cities had a small town feel.

She often daydreamed about moving away, somewhere up north where the weather was cooler. New York State. Or Illinois, even.

It was another pipe dream, of which Emily had many. Sure, she was a nurse and could find work anywhere, as could Jordan to varying degrees of success. He was an accountant after all, and who didn't need help outrunning the taxman? But his clients were *here*. Jordan had spent the last four years building a reputation, building loyalty; they would be mad to uproot it all. There was a future for the Samuels family in the not-too-shabby city of Charleston, South Carolina, and like most new parents, Emily only wanted what was best for her daughter, even if it meant those dreams of her own would never come to fruition as a result. No, moving wasn't in the cards. This small world was destined to be theirs for some time yet.

Jordan raised an eyebrow. Groaned. "So I'll take that as a 'nope, I don't have the card' then?"

"Do you love me?" Emily said, putting on her cutie-pie voice.

"I don't know," he replied, playful. "Do I?"

"Do I?" chimed Lucette from the backseat, where she sat buckled into a car seat she was already close to

outgrowing. The three-year-old kicked her feet, proud as punch for joining in an adult conversation. Her favorite doll, Natalia, rested on her lap.

Jordan grabbed the steering wheel. "Let's just forget about it. It's not like he's going to read it anyway."

Yeah, you're right. But formalities, babe. Normalcy.

The car idled at the end of the driveway, the gate to their barricaded property having already swung shut behind them. Jordan flicked on the left-hand indicator.

"But I wrote a nice message to Conrad and Sally on it, too. Can you just run back in and grab it?"

"Card! Card! Card!" Lucette yelped.

"See? Even our darling girl thinks Daddy should run back inside and get it," Emily said, touching her husband's thigh. "It's in the study right on the desk. Next to the present itself."

"You forgot that, too?"

"I know. I'd forget my own head if it wasn't screwed on. But I'm tired. The heat has really thrown my sleeping pattern out of whack."

"You, babe, have a hangover." Jordan clapped his hands together. "Booya! Man, it feels so good to see the shoe on the other foot." He switched the radio on and music filled the cramped interior of the car. "Em', every time I hear this song I'm going to think of this moment."

"I do *not* have a hangover. Turn it down."

"Oh, I beg to differ. You *downed* that wine last night."

"I drank just as much as you, thank you."

"Yep, and ever since a certain somebody came into our lives, you've become a total light-weight." He gave her a poke. "Say it and I'm out of this car in two seconds flat."

Emily put all of her might into a dramatic sigh, one that would have given the local repertory club a run for its money. "Okay. Maybe I have a little bit of a hangover."

"Hangover!" Lucette echoed.

Emily faced her husband. "Now look what you've done." She softened, leaned over, the leather seats groaning, and planted a kiss on Jordan's lips. The toothbrush bristle of the moustache he was attempting to grow tickled the underside of her nose. Emily raised a hand and impersonated their daughter waving, a pretty-as-a-picture clenching of the fingers.

Jordan—working that equally adorable smile of his, the one that made the dimples she'd fallen in love with zing into prominence—gave her a salute and stepped out into the summer heat that lent him his tan. The door thumped shut. He wiggled his ass at her in the mirror.

"Your dad's one cheeky monkey," Emily said to her three-year-old. Over Lucette's shoulder she could see Jordan stepping up to the bars of the gate to punch in their security code. Emily felt a familiar twist of the knife each and every time she laid eyes on the barricade separating the safety of her family from a world that was so much more dangerous than she'd ever anticipated it could be. And the blade of that knife had been dipped in the vinegar of loss. It burned. She mourned for the carefree days she'd had as a child, days her daughter may never have the opportunity to experience.

Little Lucette would grow up surrounded by gates and escorts, and when she was old enough to go out on her own, she'd carry an alert—what they used to call a 'rape whistle' back when Emily was growing up. It was such an unavoidable, adult concept. But something science couldn't justify had taken a bite out of the apple of their innocence. And at the end of the day, it would be Lucette's generation left hungry. Considering this, Emily thought her resentment wasn't entirely without justification.

She faced the road.

They lived on the city's northern outskirts and the isolation this provided was a double-edged sword. The quiet was wonderful; the nearest neighbors, the Crookenbacks, were a three-minute stroll down the street. On the other hand, it also meant they had to travel far for groceries, gas, and to see friends.

Well, maybe I'm okay with that. Small doses. Conrad's okay, I guess. But Sally's too churchy for me. And damn, what a gossip.

Emily switched off the radio, ran her fingers through her hair. Scratched. She needed to change shampoos, the brand she was using made her scalp itch. Her skin had always been on the sensitive side, so something with a lower pH level might be more appropriate.

This small, insignificant desire for something better would scurry back into her mind the following day, as she bent over the washtub in the back laundry, cleansing blood from her blouse. It, like so much else, would reduce her to weeping.

"You okay back there, bub?" Emily asked.

Lucette didn't reply so much as yawn.

"No, no. No sleeping, I'm sorry." Emily felt bad giving her daughter's foot a caress, one that was strong enough to make those eyes of hers open again. But nap times had to be scheduled and adhered to. Any derailment resulted in either undue sleep-ins, or worse, pre-dawn rising.

With Lucette roused, Emily reached into the backpack she took with her on outings and rummaged through loose diapers, pacifiers, and stuffed toys for the boxed juice she'd slipped in there before leaving. A just-in-case natural sugar hit for moments like this. As Emily dug, her eyes rose to the dashboard where the little hula girl in the grass skirt was stuck, rocking her Hawaiian hips, ever the beach-bound provocateur. It was the souvenir from the honeymoon that never happened, but which, all going to plan, someday would.

When the finances were right.

When they knew it was *safe*.

The dewy surface of the juice box could be felt at the bottom of the bag. Emily laced her fingers around its corners and yanked it out.

"Here we go, sw— "

Emily broke off mid-sentence, her arm half-extended. The air curdled, and as she breathed it in, it seemed to expand within her lungs. Hurt. Choked.

Through the rear window of the car she could see the side door of their single-story brick house. It was ten yards away. The hot westward wind blew, throwing flower spores through the air. They twirled, danced, their unpretentious beauty a direct contrast to her blood-splattered husband. He wrestled a naked man on the grass.

The juice box slipped from Emily's grip. Lucette gave a cry, her sweet treat having been snatched away from her.

"Jordan!"

Emily unlatched her belt, flung the door open. Extreme heat blasted, burning on contact. Bullets of sweat rolled down her neck as she ran through that sickened air, around the back of the car to the gate.

Her hands at her mouth. A ball of panic snuggled inside.

Jordan's white Polo shirt—the one she'd bought for him on Father's Day, the one that she'd picked off the rack because she knew it would show off the contours of his pecs—was no longer white. It was red. As red as the mouth of the naked man hovering over him. Emily saw the gash at her husband's neck, right near the shoulder, the ripped tendons torn and flailing as though another hand had grown there, one that was waving yet another goodbye.

She hit the pin-pad's CLOSE key and stepped beside the seven-foot-tall fence, ensuring the gate didn't side-swipe her as it shut. Were the bone-eater to take Emily as it had her husband, at least Lucette would be safe within the car on the other side.

But what if I die? What if Jordan does, too?

Emily had an answer for that one, too.

The Crookenbacks walk this road multiple times a day. Their doctor told them to exercise more, and they have been! They stopped to chinwag just last Sunday, remember? You were out here at the time, fishing bills from the blue mailbox.

The mailbox Jordan had decorated with a stick-figure family. Mom, Dad, and Bub etched in yellow paint.

Yes, Emily prayed. *The Crookenback's will come. Just please, don't let it come to that.*

The gate clicked into place, locked—as did her plan. She wouldn't run to her husband empty handed. Jordan had been doing some landscaping the prior afternoon, and had left a wheelbarrow and shovel by the flowerbed. Emily had scolded him for leaving it out at the time. "I'm all for roses, Jordan. Just put your stuff away, okay? It makes the place look messy. The Crookenbacks will see it all when they go on their walk. They always peer in."

He'd looked so handsome there in the twilight, dirt on his face. Even with the stupid moustache that wore him and not the other way round. Even though she was annoyed. But staying mad at him had been too difficult. It always was. Love was better.

Jordan's screams stretched on.

Heart pounding, mouth dry, she ran to the flowerbed and picked up that shovel, a splinter spearing the palm of her hand and going unnoticed. Emily's adrenalin shifted into overdrive.

How on earth did it get in here? The perimeter is fully secured. Or at least it should be.

"Hey!" she yelled at the creature, standing her ground and holding the tool like a spear. The viciousness of Emily's voice shocked all three of them.

Because Emily wasn't a violent person.

Never in her life had she seriously hurt another living thing, except for once when she was a teenager, the night she'd struck a possum while driving her father's car to the Dairy Queen where she worked. The animal had dodged out from between two trees, a white blur in the headlights, clipping the grill. Emily had screeched to a halt and saw the possum on its back, its broken legs kicking. Still alive. Disgusted by what mercy dictated she must do, she opened the trunk and took out the tire iron her father kept in there.

For emergencies.

She beat the possum to death and went to work with red splotches and possum fur across her uniform. There she broke down.

Emily clenched the shovel now and called her husband's name. The vibrations in her throat reminded her that yes, this really *was* happening. And that yes, there was the potential for violence in all things. Even her.

She'd seen enough infection-orientated documentaries to realize that this was a textbook attack. The zombie wanted one thing: to devour the bones of *living* humans. Authorities had tried dead animals, live ones too, with no success. This had been a phenomenal realization, one that echoed in Emily's mind in a David Attenborough-esque voice-over: *"Thus, the species that had mastered fire, visited the moon, and created the atom bomb, found its place at the top of the food chain compromised."*

And that last comment had almost proven correct. It took four years for the outbreak, which was suspected to have originated in Central America, to be brought under control. Time enough for millions of casualties. Time enough for the human race to trick itself into thinking they still had 'control'.

But things slipped through.

Textbook.

The preliminary bite had been to her husband's

neck, the aim being to bring him down. If she didn't act quickly, the zombie would use its calcified fingernails to slit open his arms and legs, gaining access to the goodies underneath. Alternatively, it would roll him over and rip out his spine.

The spines, said the voice over, *are their favorites.*

Emily gagged. That this could be happening in quiet Charleston struck her as impossible—let alone to them. This kind of thing happened to those who let their guards down, people who had grown complacent.

And that's not us!

Or was it?

(Did you grab the card, babe?)

That simple, innocuous question rung again. A death knoll.

Perhaps they *had* grown complacent, snug within domesticated denial. The bank-owned home; the car (such good mileage!); beautiful Bub, who —if all went as planned—would have a brother or sister within a few years' time; their visits to see friends for birthday parties; babysitters; news rants; wives harping at their husbands for not putting away their tools—

Emily clenched the shovel. Roared.

She jumped, aiming for the zombie's head but striking its shoulder instead, snapping the collarbone. It shot its glare at her, eyes glassy and black. They didn't blink. Emily watched its skeleton contort beneath the drum-tight pull of its skin. It looked so frail; only it wasn't. But worst of all was the way the muscles around its mouth had drawn back in a permanent smile, revealing all those elongated teeth.

A *smiler*. A *bone eater*. A *zombie*. No matter what it was called, the outcome was the same. Jordan was bleeding, and if he was bleeding—

(don't say it!)

—then he would, in time, become one of them.

Emily swiped again, connecting with the side of the creature's head. A chunk of decomposing flesh with an ear attached slapped the earth, maggots flew through the air. The man rolled off her husband's chest. Blood jetted across Emily's sneakers.

The bone eater thrashed, long legs kicking, revealing the nub of its cock and withered balls. That's where Emily aimed her next swing. *Thud*. She castrated it with a single arc, drew the shovel back and ground the genitals into a pulp. Inky soup ebbed from the mess left behind, slow as honey, and her victory just as sweet.

"Fuck you!" Emily screamed.

Jordan joined her side. He stunk of cut grass, copper, sweat. "Give it to me," he said, snatching the shovel. The creature pivoted up onto its haunches. It perched, frog-like, fists punching the ground. Its hands and arms were stained with earth.

You dug under the fence, Emily thought. *Like the* dog *you are.*

"Go to the car," Jordan said. "Protect our girl!"

Emily, her blouse doused red, ran for the gate, thumbed in the code. She glanced behind her and watched Jordan beating the zombie to death. At first his blows were aimless and punishing, connecting here and there, until he delivered the first debilitating carve to its neck, flipping the still snapping head back on its shoulders.

Emily almost laughed, delirious. The gate swung inwards.

Jordan knocked the man who had attacked him flat onto its ass. He severed the skull from the rest of the body—brutal, crunching. It was the only way to kill them, that's what that calm and collected voice-over had whispered on those late-night documentaries. And her husband knew this because he watched them with her, the two of them laying there in bed, clicking their tongues, shaking their heads, thinking: *Well, it'll never happen to us.*

Emily stepped out onto the footpath. Turned a final time. Saw the man she loved, one of Charleston's most up-and-coming accountants, grind the creature's head to a paste.

Bone dust and flower spores.

BREAK DOWN

"**M**OM? MOM?"

Emily was on her hands and knees, searching under the bed for her other shoe amongst the dust bunnies and pre-packed suitcases when she heard her daughter's call. To some degree, she was a bit of a Doomsday Prepper. Of course, anyone who had suffered losses to the outbreak over the past decade would understand. Sure, the Ministry played a pretty song about control measures, which everybody loved to dance to, but in the back of Emily's mind there was no doubt that it would all come crashing down. One day.

If something *could* happen, it eventually *would* happen.

So Emily Samuels wasn't ashamed of those three suitcases under the bed—there was pride in batteries and canned sardines, even if the blessed of this cursed shit-hole thought otherwise. Her clumsiness, however, was a different story. That, Emily was *not* proud of. She'd half-tripped getting into bed the night before and kicked her shoe to Kingdom Come.

"Mom!" Not a question this time.

"Jesus, Lucette. I'm running late. Whatever it is,

can we talk about it when I pick you up from school this afternoon?"

"No, I have to give you this before you leave."

With an exasperated sigh, Emily lifted herself up, faced her daughter, and in doing so, happened to spot her elusive Reebok wedged under the dresser. Like socks, like the television remote, she suspected her shoes came alive at night and tripped the light fantastic, finally giving in to the exhaustion of their explorations and coming to rest in unlikely places.

"Mom, you have to take this to work with you," Lucette said, buzzing around like a mosquito that wouldn't land anywhere long enough to swat. Emily snagged the shoe and sat down on the bed to slip it on.

"What?" Emily snapped with more bite than she'd intended. Fatigue always brought the gorgon out in her, some awful creature born of the nightmares that kept her awake. "I'm sorry, darlin'. You know how much I hate being late for work. Come here. What's it you want to give me?"

Lucette hesitated, and then pulled her hands out from behind her back, presenting a jumbled origami attempt. As to what animal it was supposed to be, Emily wasn't sure. "Oh, it's lovely. You're really coming along with that."

Lucette raised an eyebrow, a look of skepticism that so resembled her father Emily had to turn away. "If it's *that* good then tell me what it is."

Emily stared down at the crumpled paper, trying to decipher some shape in its clefts and points. Why did kids have to insist on testing their parents like this? But then again, Emily had been the same to her folks, too. "Giraffe?"

"It's a crane, Mom." The girl stroked the paper, a makeshift pet. "I know I'm not very good. I'm working on it, though."

"It's lovely. I don't have an office or desk to sit it on. I guess I could put it in the break room."

"Oh, it's not for you. It's for the boy you told me about. Robby."

While she'd displayed *some* prudence—glazing over how the young boy contracted his infection, for example—she shouldn't have told her daughter about Robby in the first place. Confidentiality laws. But sometimes, like all nurses, Emily needed to debrief, and since she lacked adult companionship her daughter became a substitute confidant. Was that wrong? Selfish? Emily couldn't tell, or maybe she just didn't want to. Lucette was her only real friend, and there were times, just as before when she'd evoked her father's expression, when her little girl really didn't seem quite so little.

Or perhaps I just need to get back in the saddle. Christ.

The world's scary enough without *having to date.*

"I thought it might be something nice to put out in his room, to cheer him up," Lucette said. "Tell him I'll send some more once I'm better at it. Once I'm a pro."

Emily's smile was melancholic. Lucette Samuels was a flower growing through concrete, blooming into a world that had no time for pretty things anymore.

"He'll love it," she said. "He doesn't have much in his room right now, just a few comic book posters we managed to scrounge up. I'm sure he'll be pleased as punch."

"Maybe I could go visit him sometime? He'll need a friend you know."

Her daughter's compassion and generosity was almost blinding. A child's purity could be very delicate, a thing that *should* be nurtured, yes, whilst shielded at the same time.

"Darlin', the hospice isn't a place for children."

"Robby's a child and he's there."

"Yeah, but he's sick. *Everyone* there is sick."

"You're not."

"You know what I mean, young lady." She puffed out her chest, standing tall. "*I'm* a trained professional who knows how to protect myself."

"I know all the safety rules," Lucette said without a sense of play. "You drilled them into me enough times."

(*a yellow stick-figure family painted on a blue mailbox*)

"I'll think about it," Emily said.

Lucette jumped up and down, clapping her hands. "That's *not* a no."

"And it's not a yes either, but we'll discuss it." Emily tousled Lucette's hair. "Now I've got to get going. You make sure you're ready when the bus gets here."

"Okay, Mom."

"And don't you leave this house until Mr. Reynolds pulls up outside."

"I know."

"Check the windows before you go outside, and if you see anyone that seems *off*, you stay in this house. I'd rather you miss a day of school than—"

"I know, I know. You go over this with me every

single morning. Do you think I'm dumb or something?"

Emily didn't think her daughter was dumb, but she hadn't thought she and Jordan were dumb, either. She knew that the bus drivers for the district were trained to handle 'situations' if they encountered anyone infected on the route, but Emily didn't like leaving Lucette's safety in anyone else's hands. "It's important to be careful. Never forget that."

"I won't. And don't you forget to give Robby the crane, okay?"

"Promise, I'll do it first thing when I get to work." Emily kissed Lucette on the forehead, pinching her cheek. "Love you, darlin'."

"I love you too, Mommy," she replied, wiping the kiss off her skin.

In the living room, Emily shrugged on her coat, grabbed the keys from the coffee table, and slung her purse over a shoulder. She had one foot out the door when Lucette said, "Please don't forget."

"I told you, I'll be sure to give him the crane."

"Not that. Don't forget that you said we'd discuss me going to visit Robby."

Winter's breath blew at Emily's neck. The girl before her in her stocking feet seemed so trusting. Guileless. Just as she imagined Robby's must have been. Back before the night of the Halloween festival.

I've got to keep her safe. No matter what.
I have to keep her safe.

Emily sat in her car, staring at the origami crane perched on the dash like the statuette of a Hawaiian hula dancer from another time. The honeymoon that never happened; another pipedream down the drain. And no doubt, once Lucette's interest in Japan had expanded into full-blown obsession mode, there would come a conversation Emily was already dreading.

Mom, I'd really love to visit Tokyo.

It'd be such a great experience to see another country, don't you think?

But, Mom, all my friends are doing it!

To some degree the answers to these questions were already written.

We don't have the money, sweetie. Your friends' folks have good jobs; they're not slumming it like us. I know it'd be a great experience—but who can tell what outbreak security is like in other countries?

Emily shook her head, acquiescing to the terrible realization that she was turning into her own mother. The more things changed, the more they remained the same.

Raise your angels just to clip their wings later.

It was a harsh way to live, though fair—one of her mother's favorite expressions. It might as well have been etched into her tombstone.

Thankfully, the travel conversation was still far off. Emily had to get through the current workday first, and like those that had preceded it, this morning was beginning the same way. Emily had pulled into the parking lot fifteen minutes earlier, cut the engine, and started to cry. This was her new routine. She hadn't been running late for work, not really; the truth was that Emily liked to arrive half an hour early so she could spend time in the car preparing herself for the shift ahead.

Robby weighed heavy on her thoughts.

He was a bright boy, smart and funny, and Emily enjoyed being around him, but just as Lucette was never going to get to Japan, Robby was never going to become a paleontologist, or get married, or have kids of his own. All he had ahead of him was a painful death without his family by his side.

There was one silver lining in Robby's short future though: His incubation period wouldn't be long. The neglect he'd suffered, both at the hands of those who'd kicked him to the curb and that he'd self-imposed, had led to a serious case of pneumonia. His immune system was shot to hell.

Robby was already refusing solids. His hair was falling out. The night staff reported screams coming from his room. It was all there in his notes.

Emily popped open the glove compartment and drew out some napkins from the stash she'd collected from various fast-food restaurants, using them to wipe at her eyes and blow her nose. She checked her reflection in the rearview mirror, glanced out the windshield at the Right-to-Lifers, already gathered outside the hospice at this hour.

If there was one thing she truly hated about working here, it was that the parking lot was across from the facility. Sure, she'd heard there was a side entry into the building you could sleuth into, but Emily had yet to find it. Not that she minded the few extra steps; she just dreaded having to pass the protestors every day. And they were always there, rain or shine or sleet, more dependable than the mailman.

Ha. Another one of Mom's expressions.

Emily recognized a few faces in the crowd,

including the old woman who'd accosted her on her first day. But it wasn't always the same people each morning. It was almost as if they had a rotating schedule in place.

Full-time prejudice came with part-time commitments.

Emily wondered if Robby's parents were in the group today, if it was *their shift*, or if the fact that their son was now a 'guest' would keep them away. She couldn't see them, thank God. As terrible as it sounded, their absence was preferred over Robby's incarceration serving as greater motivation for their protests.

Not that I can pretend to understand how their minds work.

During the early days of the outbreak, Emily assumed those who were the most terrified of the infected and screamed the loudest for their deaths would change their tunes once someone they loved became affected. Then they would be able to put a face to the disease, realizing that the infected were just human beings, not statistics in the making. That assumption turned out to be naïve. All over the world, parents disowned children, children turned their backs on parents, spouses split. There were reports of people killed by family members simply for being *suspected* of having the zombie parasite in their veins.

Blood wasn't as thick as water, and neither was thicker than fear.

Knuckles rapped the passenger-side window. Emily gasped, followed by a shaky laugh when she saw that it was Mama Metcalf out there peering in.

"Yoo-hoo! Space for two?"

Emily motioned for her to get in, which she did. The old woman cupped her wrinkled hands over the vents for warmth. "That feels good," she said in her slow drawl. "It's only two blocks from the L station, but it's cold as a witch's tit out there and I'm a walking popsicle."

An involuntary laugh sputtered from Emily's lips, to which Mama Metcalf's reply was a blank, questioning look. Emily enjoyed the older woman's company because she obviously had no idea just how funny she was. No matter how dark the mood, this squat little stranger could elicit smiles from stone. Emily had even seen Woods buckle to Mama Metcalf's randomness.

"Well," Emily said, "you're welcome to share my warmth."

"Same here, sweetie. I saw you sitting in the car looking like somebody done pissed all in your Cornflakes. I thought maybe you could use a friend."

The heat suffused Emily's cheeks, and she wiped at her dribbling nose with another napkin. "I'm sorry, I know this isn't very professional of me."

"Ain't no shame in letting it out sometimes," Mama Metcalf said, patting her knee.

(*There's no shame in that, Robby. We all have to let it out.*)

"It's just that, you know, this job. It's—"

"It's rough. That's why there's so much turnover."

"Yeah. How long have you been volunteering for?"

"Going on four years now."

"Wow, that's impressive. What's the secret?"

Mama Metcalf scratched her chin. "For starters, I'm old. Not much I ain't already seen or had to deal with. But you'se never too old to hurt. Breaking down empties out all the bad so you can face another day." She smiled. "And it looks like you know that secret, too. You're in for the long haul, I can tell."

"Well, I appreciate the vote of confidence. Sometimes I'm not so sure. The last few days have, well, they've tested me."

"The boy."

Emily closed her eyes, nodded.

"Whole thing's a tragedy. Bad enough what happened to him, but for his folks to just dump him that way. Can't wrap my brain around it. I mean, far as I'm concerned you don't throw your kids away no matter what. Whether they're on drugs, in jail, gay, or zombie."

Laughter bubbled up again, and though Emily tried to contain it, it slipped out anyway.

Mama Metcalf took her hand. "If you think it's hard on you just imagine how *he* feels. And that's where we come in. He needs people to help him through this, people he knows he can count on. If his folks are too piss-poor to be those people, it's our job to take up the slack."

Emily smiled. *Piss-poor.* Yet another hit from The Best of Bessie Samuels, one Emily hadn't heard since she was a child herself.

"Mama Metcalf, I'm just curious, where are you from originally?"

"Little town in South Carolina called Gaffney. You probably never heard of it."

"Ha! It's home of the peach-shaped water tower. It looks like a giant ass hanging over the interstate."

"We're famous for our giant ass," Mama Metcalf

said with a wheezy laugh. "How come you know about Gaffney?"

"Because I was born and raised in Charleston, South Carolina."

"A fellow South Cackalackian! Never would have guessed. You ain't got much of an accent."

"I've been out of the South for a long time now," Emily said, not wanting to mention that she'd purposefully worked at losing her accent because she thought it made her sound like a dull-witted hillbilly. This, in spite of the revolution that had sprung up on those very streets.

"You know what they say, 'you can take the girl outta the country but not the country outta the girl'. I moved up here a few years back after I split with my old man so I could be closer to my son, Erik. 'Course, I still don't see him much as I'd like. He's got his own life. He runs a business with his husband, Paul." Mama Metcalf paused and looked sharply at Emily. "My Ervin's queer. Not that bitchy kind of queer, though. Not like Mykel."

Emily didn't even try to mask her giggles this time. It felt good, this unrestrained release. Freeing. "I can't tell you how nice it is to meet another southern lady like yourself."

"That vice is versa, sweetie. You should come by my apartment sometime for supper. I make a killer cornbread that's so good you'll swear you're back in your own mama's kitchen."

"I might have to take you up on that."

"Please do. Bring the young'un."

Emily dabbed at her eyes again. "Oh shit. Well, there's no more putting it off is there? What do you say we get inside and start this damn day?"

"You go on ahead, sweetie. I'm going to brave the cold for another minute and get me in a few puff-puffs."

The two women exited the car, Emily carrying the crane and Mama Metcalf pulling out a pack of rolling papers and a bag of loose tobacco from her purse. Emily started for the street but stopped at the curb when the older woman said, "You ever need a friend, sweetie, I'm here."

Emily smiled, said thank you, and continued across the street. The Right-to-Lifers yelled as she passed, but their hatred was like water off a duck's back.

Another expression from better times.

THE LAST ORPHAN

EMILY WATCHED ROBBY breathe.

She became conscious of the easy, natural rise and fall of her own chest, so unlike that of the boy's, whose rib cage fluttered and hitched beneath the sheets. He'd been sleeping so much since the pneumonia had taken hold, a blessing were it not for the nightmares playing out behind those eyes.

He twitched. Clenched.

Robby's phlegmy snore filled the room, reminding Emily of the way the generator on her parents' property sounded after a season of disuse, the rumbling groan as it kicked into gear. The sound used to frighten her as a kid, though she endured it because there was light at the other end. Only the abandoned machine of meat and ambition before her wasn't starting up. It was winding down. And the only thing Robby would soon know? Darkness.

She hoped.

Nobody knew if there was consciousness after the climax. Just theories and speculation. She prayed the infected slid into nothingness, an entreaty that left her kneeling at the altar of anti-faith.

Emily tiptoed to his bed and placed the origami

crane on the adjoining table. She'd tell him who it was from later. Or then again, maybe not. Separating work from her home life was difficult enough without bringing Lucette into all this sickness.

Though it wouldn't be her first time, would it?

Yeah, and look how that *turned out.*

Emily brushed the hair from Robby's forehead but stayed her hand, afraid of waking him. There were no screams today, so there was a possibility his twitches weren't evoked by nightmares. She didn't dare rob him of what might be a good dream, one in which he climbed mountains, brandishing sword sticks to battle dragons. Dinosaurs.

Like a normal boy.

Though from where she stood, there was little normality left to Robby anymore. The beginnings of his rictus grin. The whitening skin.

Let him sleep and beat the dragon, because his waking battle is one he isn't going to win.

"Seems cruel, doesn't it?"

Emily jumped as Mykel stepped up next to her.

"Jesus, you scared me," she said, keeping her own voice low. "You're a ghost the way you sneak up on people."

Mykel gave her a wink. "I hover about an inch above the floor, that's all. You know what they say about my kind, we're light in the loafers."

Her tightened jaw relaxed into a smile. Mykel could be about as sensitive as a sledgehammer, and he seemed to be in this line of work strictly for the paycheck and not out of any deep-rooted desire to help his fellow humans, but he *could* be funny. There was no denying that. Plus, like it or lump it, they were going to be working together. Hating him was far too distracting an effort.

"What seems cruel?" Emily asked.

"Letting them linger. On." The way he broke up the sentence made her queasy.

"Yeah, because giving them the best possible care and managing their pain is such a bad thing, Mykel. In some cases we're actually slowing the process."

"But maybe what we should be doing is speeding it up."

Emily frowned. "What are you talking about?"

"Come on, who are we kidding? They're all breathing corpses. We can't change the inevitable. They're all going to end up the same way. We only call them zombies after they turn, but the truth of the matter is that they already *are*. We should send for the Crowners."

"Mykel," Emily gasped. "We are *not* going to have this conversation here. Show some decorum."

"Why not? You don't think he can hear us do you? And, I mean, look how peaceful he looks. They could do it while he's sleeping and he'd be that peaceful forever."

Emily's voice was little more than a whisper. "You shouldn't be talking like that. They're still *people*. And they deserve our respect and compassion."

Mykel infuriated her further by laughing. "See, it's that kind of bleeding-heart thinking that caused so many people to try to hide infected family members in the first place. That only made the epidemic worse. 'Hiders' are just domesticated terrorists."

Emily shot at him and latched her hand to his forearm, the fingernails digging in. Mykel gawked, shocked. Her breathing was not so even and calm now. She held him for a moment longer, their eyes locked, and waited for the urge to slap him to fade. It did. Her grip slackened, leaving imprints in her co-worker's flesh, which was so much less than he deserved. Though better that than a star-shaped bruise on his face and a visit to Woods' office soon afterwards, a visit that would likely prove her last.

"Stop," was all Emily could manage.

At first Mykel didn't move or reply, his face an impassive mask. Then he smiled and said, "I knew you had some spunk in you, New Girl," before turning and exiting the room.

Emily walked down the hall, carrying a plastic tub full of supplies. Even though Corridor 3 looked like every other corridor in the building, it *felt* different. The sense of finality was stronger here, as if each death had woven itself into the space, tainting the antiseptic air, coating the walls, slicking the floors, soiling the beds. Were she to put a record needle to the walls she would no doubt hear the tin-can music of innumerable death rattles, all of those final words and prayers.

It's in your head, girl.

Only it wasn't. This was Corridor 3, The Final Stages Unit. FSU. Emily had been lucky enough to not have stepped foot in this area since her induction. But another staff member had quit that morning and Woods herself had requested Emily pick up the rounds—a backhanded display of trust if there ever was one. The kindest compliments always came with the unkindest expectations.

Emily drew herself together, concentrated on the task at hand. She gripped the tub tighter than she had Mykel's arm. Well, almost.

Out of the frying pan and into the fire. Let's do this.

The door on her left was open and inside was the patient she'd encountered on her first day, the one whose wife had called him Speedy. Emily had since learned his name was Reginald Simms. To the best of her knowledge, his wife had not visited since.

Ahead in the next room, through another open door, giggles trailed into the hallway. Emily glanced in at Mama Metcalf, sitting on a bed with a female patient, engaged in a rousing game of Uno.

"Hey sweetie," Mama Metcalf said, her voice muffled by the mask all personnel were required to wear over their noses and mouths while in the FSU. Emily was wearing a similar one herself. "Want to join us?"

"I'd love to, but I have a bed bath to give. Hi there, Ma'am. How are you doing?"

"Nurse Samuels, this is Tammy. Tammy, Nurse Samuels."

"Hi, love," their guest said. "Sure we can't tempt you with a hand?"

"Ladies, there's nothing I'd rather do. But I must soldier on."

"Just as well," Tammy said. "Mama here is beating the pants off of me. But I'm a glass-is-half-full kind of gal. I'll die before I let her win again."

Mama Metcalf and Tammy laughed again, setting off a volley of coughing in the patient. The gaunt woman hacked sputum into a kidney-shaped basin, which would later be disposed of in a hazardous waste container and incinerated.

Emily couldn't help staring. Tammy's smile was stretched so tight the yellowed teeth jutted out, lending her a mule-ish look. Emily wondered how old she was; she could be twenty or sixty. Her hairless head looked like a skull covered in the veneer of skin. Dim, hollow eyes—only a few shades lighter than those of the man who had bitten Jordan.

Yet still she joked. Still laughed.

"You need some help?" Mama Metcalf asked, starting to rise.

"Oh no, I can handle it. You two continue with your game."

"More like a massacre," Tammy said as Mama Metcalf laid down a Draw 4 card.

Emily left them laughing and continued down the hall. Tammy's half-filled glass should have lightened the atmosphere but instead left her feeling ashamed. Guilty. If someone with as many problems as Tammy could find humor in this darkness, what right did she have to wallow in self-pity?

I'm not wallowing.

(Then why all those matted Kleenex tissues in the car?)

I'm trying to make a difference.

(Oh, is that what you call it?)

I'm . . . using my own fucked up bullshit as motivation to help others.

There was truth in that, but with a lie at its center.

Her destination was at the end of the hall on the left.

The intake file, which Emily had read after being cornered by Woods, listed the guest's name as Mr. Edwin Mabry, age 47. He contracted the infection five years ago. He'd held on longer than most, though his journey was almost at an end.

Last stop Corridor 3.

Emily stepped into the room and came to an abrupt halt, almost losing purchase on the tub. It wasn't the sight of the wasted figure in the bed that startled her, but his companion. A healthy man sat in the chair next to the bed holding Mr. Mabry's hand.

"I'm sorry," Emily said. "I didn't realize any visitors had come in this morning."

The man also wore a mask, but the creases at the corners of his eyes told her he was smiling. "I've been here since last night."

"Oh, I didn't realize."

"I know it's technically against the rules, but Eddie here doesn't have much longer so the rules tend to get a little bendy. Woods cleared it. She's good like that."

"I see. I'm Nurse Samuels."

"Vick Weston." Emily recognized the name from the intake file, where he was listed as their guest's Next Of Kin.

"I'm supposed to give Mr. Mabry his bed bath."

"Go right ahead."

Emily walked over to the bed and placed the tub of supplies on the table. After washing her hands at the sink, she donned a pair of latex gloves and turned back to see Vick reclining into the chair.

"Vick, I might have to ask you to step outside to allow Mr. Mabry his privacy."

"Eddie doesn't have anything I haven't already

seen. We've known each other since Junior High and I'm not leaving his side longer than it takes to go to the bathroom. Not 'til the fat lady sings."

Emily considered going to find Woods and decided against it. She'd been in this situation before in a number of hospitals and aged care villages, only this scenario was better than most. Generally speaking, when a family member requested to be present for the bathing of a loved one, the staff member in question was being watched to ensure they were doing the correct thing. In other words, they were under suspicion of wrongdoing. Not that Emily had ever been anything less than professional in her years on the field, but she couldn't be by someone's side twenty-four hours a day. Good workers could be the unfortunate beneficiaries of the bad ones. The quality of care fluctuated from worker to worker with frightening elasticity.

And the bad workers could be *very* bad.

But Emily could tell from the man's warmth that she wasn't being scrutinized. That wasn't what this was about. Vick's desire to be present was about companionship, not accruing evidence for a Ministry complaint.

"Mr. Mabry," Emily said. The man in the bed didn't stir or open his eyes. An IV stuck into his left arm dripped morphine into his system that would ease the pain as much as possible. He was also hooked to a machine that monitored his vitals, what those on the floor called a 'nurse on a stick'. It displayed his elevated heart rate and blood pressure. It was high. Too high. Perspiration dappled his face, his temperature hovering just over 100 degrees.

"Mr. Mabry, I'm going to remove your gown and wash you now, okay?"

"I'm not sure if he can hear you, Ms. Samuels."

"Probably not," Emily said, her voice calm and kind. "It's just me paying my respects, keeping Mr. Mabry's dignity."

She didn't disclose to him that she'd also been taught in nurses' school to continue addressing a patient in the same way even *after* they died. That, Emily suspected, Vick didn't need to hear. The fat lady still had a few songs left in her repertoire yet.

Emily lifted his upper torso and untied the gown's string at the back of his neck.

Vick stood. "Need a hand?"

"It's okay, I've got it," she said. This wasn't just bravado. While two people were required to bathe an unresponsive patient, Mr. Mabry weighed so little it was like lifting a scarecrow that had fallen off its post. Only this guest wasn't made from hay clippings and sawdust, just good old-fashioned skin and bone. Nor would it scare those birds away, either. If anything, the smell of its rot would draw them in, their shadows pin-wheeling over the fields as they swooped to feed. Bellies full of carrion. Lunatic squawks.

Vick came over anyway and started undoing the snaps at the shoulders.

Emily nodded, accepting his help. Care givers needed to care, it was as simple as that, and she thought it wrong to stand in the way of that. Given time—and from the look of it not much—Death would be the one to sever that relationship, and when it did, Vick would adopt the empty glare of those forced to live without purpose. Emily had witnessed this too many times.

With the gown removed and tossed in the bin, the two lowered Mr. Mabry back onto the bed, drawing back the covers. She took a moist wipe from the pack, folded it, and began stroking it across his forehead, in the hollows of his eyes.

Vick held out a hand. "Pass me one of those. I'll start on his arms."

She handed him a pair of disposable gloves, which he declined. "I hate those things." Emily noticed the delicate way he lifted the right arm, swabbing the pit.

"You're good at that," she said. "Keep that up and we might have to get you on the ward."

"Ha-ha, thanks but no thanks. I've taken care of enough sick people in my time. This is my last vigil."

Emily detected the sadness in his voice and decided not to pursue the subject further. Once she was done with Mr. Mabry's face, she tossed the wipe, got a fresh one, and started on the left arm, being careful not to dislodge the IV.

"So there's no other family in the picture, is that right?" Emily asked.

"No family that cares."

"That's sad to hear, Vick."

"Trust me when I say you're never too old to be orphaned. We learned that lesson the hard way. There was a group of us. When we were all together we were stronger than steel and that was enough."

Emily smiled as they both wiped down Mr. Mabry's chest and stomach area. "That sounds nice. Are the other people in the group going to come and visit?"

"They're all dead."

"Oh, I'm so sorry. That was silly of me to say."

"What can you do? It happens to us all. There's no fighting it. They were all infected except me."

Emily cleared her throat and plucked a fresh wipe from the packet. "Excuse me, Mr. Mabry. I'm just going to bathe your downstairs area, okay?" When she had first become a nurse, cleaning genitals embarrassed her. Now she did it with the detached precision the job required.

"There's only Eddie and me left," Vick said, starting on his friend's right leg. "And soon, there'll just be me. The last orphan."

Emily had no words of comfort so she said nothing at all.

Vick started washing Mr. Mabry's feet. It reminded Emily of something from the Bible, scenes she'd half-forgotten from her years in church with her parents, their knees flush against the pews, all of them overlooked by a statue of their tortured cross-maker. Why celebrate religion when you could grieve it, right?

"He died for our sins," her mother would say. "Be grateful for what you've got."

Guilt.

Guilt so strong and prideful not all the moist wipes in the world could wash it away.

Emily kept her silence, recognizing the man's need to unburden. Part of being a nurse wasn't just caring for the patient's physical needs but his mental and emotional needs as well. Sure, Vick wasn't her patient, but that didn't mean he wasn't in need of some healing. Everyone, after all, longed to be listened to.

It reminds us that we're alive.

"It was our own fault, really," Vick said. "We were carnal." He sighed. "And careless."

"Though not you?" Emily asked, rolling Mr. Mabry onto his side. Vick held him in place as Emily cleaned the man's back and buttocks.

"Believe me, I wasn't spared because I employed restraint or good judgment. Some days I think I was spared so I could care for them all, which is the kind of thought that helps me sleep. On other days, the really bad ones, I just wonder if it wasn't plain old *bad luck* I escaped infection."

He didn't say any more until after Emily had finished the bed bath. He spoke again as he held Mr. Mabry in a sitting position and Emily put a fresh robe on him. "You know, some people actually have the audacity to tell me that *I'm* the fortunate one."

Most wouldn't understand how cruel such a statement was; only Emily did. Or at least she *thought* she did. Were someone to ask her that day if there were any more lessons for her to learn about the pain of survival, Emily would have laughed them off.

And she would have been wrong. She just didn't know it yet.

Emily gathered up her supplies and trash, and left the two men together. Mykel was waiting for her in Corridor 3. He walked with her, opening the door to the Sluice room, where she then deposited the waste into a hazardous material bin and placed the bedpan into the washing machine. She thumped its metallic jaws shut and turned to face him.

"What do you want, Mykel?"

"I just don't understand that, New Girl."

"Understand what?"

"That man in there. I couldn't help overhearing. If I had to watch all my friends die because they couldn't keep it in their pants, I'd be down on my knees thanking the big fella upstairs every night I was lucky enough to escape safe."

Emily pushed by him and re-entered the corridor. They buzzed through the security door and stepped into the adjoining wing. "In my book, alive is always better than dead," Mykel said, squeezing antiseptic wash over his hands. "No exceptions."

"Is there anything else you'd like to say? We've got a job to do. Five more sponges, twelve assisted feeds, beds to make, and notes. Time is money, Mykel, and you're wasting both standing there."

"There is, actually. Woods wants to see you."

Without acknowledging him, Emily wormed her way back to Woods' office. As she did so, she fished through the pocket of her pants and slid out her phone to check the time. This Emily did on the sly, as it was against facility policy to have non-approved communication devices on the floor. Emily saw the six missed calls from Saint Mary's.

Her phone had been on silent all morning.

Emily found Woods standing behind her desk. Officious. Waiting.

"What's wrong?" Emily asked.

"There's someone from your daughter's school on line one. Seems there's been some trouble."

INTERLUDE THREE

Open the highest wing, bring it upwards and press the sides of the paper inwards at the same time. Flatten it down, and again, crease well.

EMILY PULLED THE needle through her husband's skin and yanked the thread. The jack-o-lantern wound pinched inwards, sealed. Jordan flinched, his teeth gritted together. He was on his side, splayed across the couch, which Emily had covered with the plastic tarp they'd used to paint Lucette's bedroom. Blood pooled in its crinkles. Debris from her makeshift triage surrounded them, all those matted cotton buds, tweezers, gauze, saline solution.

An empty bottle of whiskey. They had been saving it for a special occasion.

Lucette was locked in her room with enough crayons and toys to keep her occupied. She was happy in there, and wouldn't be able to hear her father's groans over the television in the living room. Midday cartoons blared violence as cats mangled dogs with hammers. Only these animated beings didn't bleed. Just stars and birds flying about their heads.

Now that the bite had been tended to as best Emily could without taking Jordan to the hospital, they sat on the couch, held each other tight, and sobbed. Their misery was pure and undiluted and shameless. Her hands gripped his arms. Jordan gripped her back. They were pieces of the same shattered Humpty Dumpty, and sadly, as was the case in Lucette's picture books, not even the King's horses and men would be able to put them back together again.

"Don't let me go," Jordan said. His breath was sour. It smelled of dirt.

"I won't, darlin'. I promise." She rocked him.

"I'm so fucking scared."

"Me too." Emily kissed his forehead. He was hot to the touch.

Emily pulled the needle through Natalia, her daughter's doll, and yanked the thread. The black button eye drew back into place. "There you go," Emily said, handing the toy over. It was seven-thirty in the evening, Jordan was already passed out in their bedroom, and it was time for Lucette to turn in. The little girl took the doll in her arms and held it to her chest.

"Sweetheart," Emily began, steeling herself. "I need to talk to you. A big girl talk, okay?"

"Okay, Mom. I'm a big girl."

"You sure are. And I'm so proud of you, too. You know that, right?"

"Yep! Just like I'm proud of Natalia," Lucette said. "She keeps me safe at night."

"Does she? She's a good dolly." Emily ruffled the old toy's plaits. "But let's be serious now."

"We're listening, aren't we?" Lucette gestured to

the dusty old toy, squeezed its neck, and made it nod. Emily half smiled.

"That's good, sweet*heart*."

Her last word fissured in two, shattering the dignity Emily had been fighting to maintain. She fumbled through the pockets of her jeans for a tissue. There were none left. Emily let the briny tears free-flow, a greasy layer on her skin.

She studied her daughter in the star shaped illumination of the slowly turning night-light. The blue glow crept across Lucette's face, followed by shadow, though Lucette's eyes shimmered throughout, like the evening sky reflected in the bottom of twin wells.

And every bit as deep.

"Don't be sad, Mom," she whispered. Her chubby fingers reached across the duvet to curl about Emily's wrist. "There, there. There, there."

Lucette propped herself up on one elbow and offered the toy to her mother. "I'll share with you. It's good to share, isn't it? Maybe Natalia can keep us *all* safe."

With a finger, Emily traced the stitching she'd threaded. The black button eyes, unlike those belonging to her daughter, held no vivacity. They were stoic, like those of the bone eater that had dug under their fence and attacked her husband.

The stars continued to fall around them.

"Lucette. Your father and I always taught you that it was bad to lie."

"Ah-huh. It's naughty. And naughty girls don't get presents from Santa. He's always watching."

Emily, chewing on her lower lip, couldn't help guffawing at the depths she, as an adult, had gone to swindle her child into virtue. It went beyond hypocrisy. Fat Saint Nick with his bag of bribes was yet another deception that kept the New Developed World spinning on its axis. Such trickeries, they all thought, kept the infection away. In the slums. Where it belonged.

Sweetheart, we're in here. *The monsters are out* there.

It won't happen to us.

"Natalia can't keep us safe." Emily's voice was stern, maybe too stern, but it *had* to be. It was time to be what her own mother always said: *harsh, but fair*. "If we want to be safe we have to look after one another. Do you understand what I'm saying?"

The three-year-old nodded. Those wet eyes of hers continued to glimmer, but now it seemed that something was shifting within them, right there at the bottom of the wells. A serpentine creature, ugly and adult.

This was its birth.

Emily took another breath before continuing. "There's no such thing as Santa. He's made up. I'm so sorry, sweetheart. But sometimes it's *okay* to lie. Sometimes it's the only way we get by. And I need you to listen to me now. You need to understand that this is the most important talk we'll ever have."

"Okay, Mommy."

"Lucette, your Daddy and I need you to lie."

Emily pulled the needle through the tarpaulin and yanked the thread, sealing the makeshift body bag that held the bone eater's remains. The stars above were not those from Lucette's night-light, these were real constellations. Emily wanted to assimilate herself amongst those distant balls of gas, burning for generations on end, shedding little in the way of light, and unsympathetic to the wishes cast upon them.

How sweet it would be right now to feel nothing.

This didn't happen, though. There was no clemency. She was, and always would be, anchored to this delusional planet. To this hurt.

Somebody up there, please help us.

We're dying down here. Can't you see that?

Our land is honeycombed with tombs, and it'll crumble under our feet one day. Soon.

I'll build a bridge from me to you out of corpses. Just promise me you'll be there when I arrive. You need to pinkie-swear I won't be alone.

The sky held no answers.

So Emily shoved the bulging bag into the pit she'd dug in the backyard instead. It thumped against the soil, exhaustion threatening to drag her in with it. Emily pushed through. With her sweaty clothes sticking to her flesh like a second skin, with the mosquitos swarming about her face, she heaved dirt. Over and over again.

There was no breeze. No moon.

She was done.

Emily showered inside while bulb-happy moths beat themselves to a powdery death against the bathroom window. Emily toweled off, wrapped herself in the dressing gown she'd left by the clothes basket that morning and walked to her bedroom door.

Stopped.

Emily could hear Jordan's breathing. She began to

shake; terrified of the darkness that would come when she switched off the hallway sconces, and the darkness waiting inside her room. Emily stepped away from the door, and in doing so, learned to hate herself.

She tiptoed into the study. Flipped the lock. Folded in on herself. The floor was cool against her cheek. Kevin's birthday card and present were still on the desk.

The lies she'd rooted in her daughter's head echoed through her ears.

If anyone asks, your Daddy has gone away for work. He'll be gone a while. Don't tell anyone anything. *This will be our secret. Just you, me, and Natalia. And you're not going to be going to daycare for a while because you're 'sick'. That's what we'll say.*

Everything's going to be okay.

SWEARWORDS AND PEANUT BUTTER CUPS

LUCETTE SAT ON the edge of the bed with her hands in her lap, dressed for the day. There had been a time—and not so long ago it seemed—when she did this and her feet didn't touch the floor. Now they did. This made her sad. Not sad in the way some cartoons did, or like the time the only real friend she'd had, Imogen, moved to New York with her parents. This sadness was new, different from those difficult-to-define barbs she thought of as memories of her father. Lucette missed the way her legs used to swing back and forth, and being unable to do so made her feel older than she wanted to be. She was sad because nobody had asked if she wanted to grow up in the first place.

If Mom is anything to go by, being an adult doesn't look like fun. Getting old means you have to yell a lot and be angry over every little thing.

Every fucking *thing.*

Lucette glanced about the room, half expecting the walls of their apartment to split apart, revealing a network of ears and eyes in the crawlspace instead of the insulation that failed to keep them warm at night. These would be her mother's spies—the secret ones trained in the ancient art of overhearing naughty thoughts, every single swear word. Teachers, on the other hand, didn't require such allies. And why would they when the world was full of tattletales?

No. I'm being stupid. There are no spies. I think another part of getting older is learning how to read little girls' minds. But if that's the case, then why can't Mom tell I didn't mean to be bad?

I don't even know why I did what I did.

Her hands gripped the backpack sitting beside her on the mattress. She lowered her head. Yes, perhaps it was best not to swear, even if it was only a thought, until her mother had cooled down.

And she hasn't. Nope. I can tell because of the way she's banging things. She does that when she's angry. Slamming cupboards. Clunking dishes. Thumping about.

Those thumping footsteps drew closer to Lucette's door, a dread-inducing moment she knew would come. Her heart pattered; wild butterflies she knew could never be netted danced in her stomach.

The walls of Lucette's bedroom were lined with boyband and baseball posters. Those handsome faces stared now, beckoning invitations into their respective worlds.

Hurry, they seemed to say, *before your mother has a chance to open the door! Escape with us.*

Lucette imagined diving into the crowd of cheering girls as the band played on the stage. There would be flashing lights and cavity-sweet melodies. Or maybe running out onto the diamond pitch would be safer? She had a pretty good right-hand swing on her, even if she hadn't practiced since summer. The baseball bat would feel great in her hands, yet not half as good as connecting it with the ball. *Thonk!* Here, the crowd cheered for her, not the other way round—

The bedroom door opened. Her mother stood there, handbag tucked under one arm. Keys in hand. "It's time to go," the grownup said.

Still angry.

Lucette didn't dare a thought, stood.

Their car grumbled down the street as though it were crafted from the same wound-up anger as her mother. Lucette wondered how much longer the 'silent treatment' was going to continue. She wasn't even allowed to turn on the radio. There was only the whine of the air conditioning, the blaring of passing vehicles, sounds that in their own unique way confirmed how much trouble she was in.

Lucette stared through the window instead, watching the sky change color from a bruise to a faint pink that reminded her of the icing on her last birthday cake. Like her feet touching the floor, like summer, it didn't seem so long ago. And yet everything was different now.

The sun hauled itself up and the light stung her eyes. Enough was enough.

"I'm sorry," Lucette said again in the coy way that sometimes helped her get what she wanted. "Don't be mad at me. Please."

"I'm not mad," Emily said, drumming her fingers on the steering wheel. "I'm disappointed."

Lucette sighed and made herself a promise: when she was old enough to be a mother, she would never say that to her own children (of which there would be three, she'd decided, all girls, their names being Cindy, Lindy, and Sue). The 'disappointment' line hurt in ways Lucette suspected adults had long ago forgotten.

"I just wanted those kids to stop picking on me,"

Lucette said. "I didn't know I was going to get kicked out of school."

"Don't be over-dramatic. You weren't kicked out of school. You were suspended. Which is bad enough."

Lucette quieted and gazed back through the glass. Over the top of the passing buildings, she tracked a flock of geese flying in perfect formation toward the emerging sun as if seeking incineration. Her mother appeared to be driving with similar conviction. Lucette was positive they would both burn just so the point was proven.

I was bad. I know that now. Can't we skip to the part where we're happy again?

"You know they called me at work, right?" Emily said, each word a lashing.

Why does Mom always ask questions she already knows the answers to?

"Yeah."

"You're lucky my boss is so understanding. We'd be screwed if she wasn't."

Lucette had been hauled into the principal's office only the day before, and there, forced to wait until her mother arrived—an excruciating two hours in which she played out a dozen punishment scenarios ranging from confiscated toys to medieval torture devices, like the ones they had learned about in school last year. Contraptions with spikes and spokes. Sitting there, having survived Principal Higgins' yells, Lucette assumed that things could not get any worse.

Wrong.

Geese, take me with you. I'm sure I'll be a good flyer. I'd rather have the sun over this.

Her mother continued. "You pretended to be a *you-know-what* and tried to bite three students."

"They were picking on me. They said you were a zombie lover."

"And they're being reprimanded for doing so. Not that their punishment fits the crime, mind you. Two days of afternoon detention—can you believe it? That Higgins is a fucking joke."

They pulled up at a stoplight.

"Swear word, Mom."

The taillights of the car in front cast a faint red glow over her mother's face. A few stray snowflakes lit on the windshield.

"Don't, Lucette. Don't. You started a panic. You were moaning, lurching around. Some of the other kids thought you were infected for real. That's why Higgins suspended you until the end of the quarter. He doesn't want to see either one of us until after New Year; though I suspect he'd rather we not come back at all. He suggested I, oh, how did he put it? Yes. 'Find a more appropriate placement' for you. A private academy. Is that what you want? You'd miss all of your friends."

"No I wouldn't," Lucette snapped. "I don't really have any friends. Imogen's long gone."

That grown up face turned to her again, coinciding with the car ahead accelerating down the road, whisking away its red light. Lucette drew her backpack tight. "I know I did wrong, Mom. I was just so angry. I don't care that you're a—"

(Fucking)

"—zombie lover. I like that you help people, even if others don't. They're stupid."

They were close to her mother's work now. Lucette wanted to cry but tried to be a big girl. "I'm sorry I said 'zombie'."

They didn't speak again for another three blocks. Traffic was heavy.

"Standing up for yourself isn't a bad thing, Lucette. You've just got to go about it the right way. If anyone gives you heat, you talk to me first. Understood?"

"Crystalline," Lucette said, a word that she didn't completely understand, but one that she'd heard her mother say many times over. It felt right here. Honest.

"Lucette, I'm stressed. Let's go over the rules, okay? Assure me you know them by heart. You haven't forgotten them since last night, have you?"

"*No.*"

"Sorry. Can you answer me again? Without the attitude this time."

"No."

"That's better. We're almost there. Tell me what I want to hear so I can feel better about this."

The snow was falling heavier now.

"I'm not to leave the break room," Lucette said.

"Right, not even to go out the door into the courtyard. It's cold out there, and the last thing I need is for you to get sick."

"Is there a TV in the break room?"

"There is. I'm not sure it works, though."

"Well, can I borrow your phone to watch stuff?"

"No, Lucette. This isn't a vacation. You've got plenty to keep you occupied in your pack. Books, drawing paper, crayons."

"But I'm going to get bored."

"Well, young miss, you should've thought of that before you displayed such disrespectful behavior."

"I didn't really bite anyone. Nobody got hurt."

"Darlin', the infected aren't fairytale monsters. They're people who are sick."

"I know that."

"Yeah, I doubt that. Actually, spending time at the hospice is going to teach you a few lessons, I think. It'll show you the value of respect. The infected shouldn't be made fun of or treated as jokes."

"That wasn't what I was doing. And I promise I'll be good."

"By *good* I hope you mean quiet and out of the way."

"Yes," Lucette said. "But I still get to meet Robby, right?"

A beat. "I don't know."

"Don't punish him because I messed up."

"*Him?*"

"Robby needs a friend, right?"

They pulled up into a parking lot, passing a crowd of people holding signs near the curb. "I have to hand it to you, Lucette. You're a first-rate emotional manipulator. A pint-sized prodigy."

The car fell silent.

"Mom? Who are those people out there? They look so *angry.*"

"They're nothing but grown-up bullies. And they aren't worth the time of day." The grinding hand break; the groan of the imitation leather seats as her mother turned to face her head-on. "Are they?"

Lucette smiled. "No way, José."

***

The smell of the hospice made Lucette think of the time their class mascot, Johnny Pepperworth the hamster, died. It had been she who'd been assigned the duty of cleaning out his vacated cage. Their teacher, Mrs. Pony—or so they called her on account of her horse-like nostrils—had already removed the corpse from the room. Though to where she didn't know. Mrs. Pony came back and comforted the class as they cried. There was no shame, just well-earned sadness. Lucette and Imogen took Johnny Pepperworth's cage down to the side quadrangle, and under the supervision of an older student, upended the hay and wood shavings onto the ground and hosed them away.

A musky stink had filled her sinuses, as penetrating as onions, and just about as pleasant. Johnny Pepperworth's cage—hamster pee, neglect, and something Lucette had forgotten about, but which was coming back to her now.

The smell of dead things.

Lucette pushed this thought aside as she was led through the hospice, her mother's hand sweaty against her own. Corridors stretched off in many directions, dwindling into dark vanishing points that made those butterflies in her stomach flutter once more. It was difficult to tell if their wings were stirred by fear or excitement.

They passed infected people—'guests', as her mother insisted she consider them—Lucette doubted that was what they were. There was no bell-hop jumping out to retrieve bags in trade for tips as they did in the movies. No joy.

Just shuffling Halloween decorations come to life.

"Hello, little one," said an old bleached woman to Lucette as they walked down one of those long hallways. At first Lucette recoiled, then stilled. "Come visit later with your Mommy and read me the Tribune." Her voice was gravelly, though kind. Lucette noted her oversized smile, her knobbled fingers, the sliver of spittle slithering to the floor. The aide by the old woman's side ushered her away, taking with her some of that distinct Johnny Pepperworth smell.

They passed a common area where a woman with a guitar was singing to guests propped up in their seats like rows of unmoving dolls in a storefront window. There were no cheers or applause as there had been in Lucette's concert fantasy.

I wouldn't clap, either. Jeez. That lady's a terrible singer!

On some level, Lucette knew she should be afraid of this place, with its tall ceilings and off-white walls. Afraid of the woman who had reached out for her, or any one of the dozen others she'd locked eyes with. But there was no fear, at least not as much as she'd assumed there would be. Lucette had almost screamed with panic when her mother explained that there was no other alternative—she would have to stay at the hospice for a while, like it or not. Only now that Lucette was here she wondered what all of her fuss had been over.

It's just a place where people help other people. Right?

They entered the break room, which was small and cramped. It was empty except for a refrigerator, microwave, coffeemaker, two vending machines, notices of every color over the walls, and a table setting. There was a door leading off to a courtyard where the snow was falling. Lucette had no intention of venturing there.

"Take a seat," Emily instructed as she rifled through Lucette's backpack, retrieved her lunchbox, and put it in the refrigerator. A clock ticked from above the wall near a digital screen with numbers flashing on it.

"What's that, Mom?"

"That? It's a room alert. It flashes when a guest presses their bedside call-button."

"So someone's going to see them? Like, right now."

"I hope so."

"Do they have to wait long?"

Her mother closed the refrigerator door and about turned, hands on hips. "Sometimes too long."

"Well, hello there," said a tall black lady in white scrubs from the doorway.

"Mrs. Woods, this is my daughter, Lucette," Emily said. " Lucette, this is my boss."

"Nice to meet you."

"And you as well. Your mother's told me a lot about you. "

Lucette felt her mother's hand on her shoulder. "Mrs. Woods, I just want to thank you again for letting me bring her. Just until I can sort something else out."

"It's fine. As I said yesterday, this isn't the first time we've had little ones here at work. If anything, it brightens the place up. I've had to bring my boys in more than once."

"I promise, it's only until I can find a day-sitter, or day-care, or, well, something."

"It won't be easy, as I'm sure you've guessed. Not

when people find out where you work. An unfortunate prejudice we have to deal with." Mrs. Woods gave Lucette an unreciprocated smile. "But the year's almost through. It'll be Christmas before you know it and you'll be on holidays, Emily."

"Thanks for approving my leave so fast. This situation, obviously, wasn't planned."

"Don't tell the others I said this, but we work to live, not live to work." Mrs. Woods crossed her arms. "If we forget that, we tend to slip up. I don't like slip-ups. Just so long as you can work both Christmas and New Years' Day mornings we've got a deal. I've got hardly anybody willing to take those shifts."

"I won't let you down."

Lucette took out her crayons and drawing paper, pretending she wasn't listening, even though she was. The two adults in the room acted as though she weren't present, let alone discussing the inconvenience she was putting them all through. But there were advantages to keeping quiet; one of the many ways of attaining knowledge was to become invisible and let the real world play out. Sometimes being a witness was a little like being a student. Today was one such time.

Emily knelt next to her. "I have to get to work, darlin'. I'll be by to look in on you before you know it."

"And my office is just across the hall," Mrs. Woods said. "I'll be in there most of the day doing paperwork. If you need anything, knock away. Might even put you to work!"

Once Lucette had been left alone, the silence of the break room settled over her. She tried to draw, only her mind was as blank as the sheet. Her attention kept returning to the digital display above the door. F-17, it still read in scarlet lettering.

It blinked down at her, a conspiratorial red eye.

She looked at the clock, shuddered. Fingers of unease wrapped around her limbs, pulling away the layers of her warm clothing to let in the chill. The person in F-17 had been buzzing for almost twenty minutes now.

No, not person. 'Guest'.

Yeah, right.

Lucette thought that if she continued to look at the alert she could *will* it into being answered, though that didn't seem to be working at all. Soon, another room number flashed up alongside it, this one reading B-2.

Followed soon by another.

D-5.

B-1.

RESP-2.

Every flash, a cry for help.

It didn't end there. More and more they came—and faster, too—until the display was nothing more than an overlapping sequence of blinking numbers and letters, a kind of confused countdown. It was then, and only then, that Lucette became afraid.

"Hey there," came a female voice from a new face striding into the break room. "You must be Emily's young'un."

"Yes, ma'am. I'm Lucette."

"You can call me Mama Metcalf."

The woman walked over to the fridge and placed a brown paper bag inside, its bottom discolored by grease stains. Then she stepped over to the snack machine, dropped in a dollar and punched the keypad, a four-pack of peanut butter cups sliding out and falling into the chute.

"Should you be eating that?" Lucette asked.

Mama Metcalf plucked at the edges of the package, tearing it open. "What do you mean?"

"I don't know; my mother always tries to get me healthy food. I figured all nurses were that way."

"I've known some 300 pound nurses that'd blow that theory right outta the water," Mama Metcalf said with a laugh. "Besides, I ain't a nurse, just a volunteer. So I can eat all the junk I want."

As if to emphasize the point, she popped one of the peanut butter cups in her mouth. "Christmas is right around the corner. You excited?"

Lucette nodded.

"What'd you ask Santa for?"

"Santa isn't real, Mama Metcalf."

The old woman cocked her head and sat down at the table next to her, sparing a quick glance at the half-hearted drawings Lucette had scribbled into existence. "Maybe there's no fat old coot who flies around dropping presents down chimneys, but he exists in the 'Christmas spirit'."

"I guess. Anyway, I told my mom I want a cell phone. She says I'm too young."

"Well, Emily probably knows best."

"Did you have a cell phone when you were my age?"

Mama Metcalf laughed again, spewing flecks of chocolate. "Honey, they wasn't no cell phones when I was your age. Only phone we had was a big rotary dial monstrosity, and we had to talk on the party line."

"What's a party line?"

"Never mind, you'll never have to know! Look, I can't eat any more of these things. Why don't you take the rest?"

"Ugh. My mom doesn't really like me eating that kind of stuff."

Mama Metcalf looked toward the door then leaned forward over the table, lowering her voice. "Gobble them up real quick. All girls need a secret or two."

Lucette cast her own glance at the doorway, and then snatched up the package and scarfed down the remaining two cups. An explosion of sugary goodness.

Much better than those stupid carrot sticks in my lunchbox.

Mama Metcalf took the empty package, crumpled it up, and then carried it to the trashcan. "I got to get to work. It was a pleasure meeting you."

The woman was almost out the door when Lucette called, "Mama Metcalf?"

"Yeah, honey?" she said, turning back.

"I'm sorry I told you there's no Santa. I thought you would've known by now."

CORRIDOR 3

LUCETTE FOUND IT almost silly how nervous and excited she was to meet this total stranger. But the very idea of Robby being alone in this place, abandoned by his family, unable to go out in the sun or play with friends, filled her with an aching she couldn't describe.

They passed a woman in a white hospital gown going in the opposite direction, clutching a wheeled metal pole, a bag of clear liquid hanging from the top, a tube snaking down to jab into her arm. Her hair was straw yellow, so thin her sore-covered scalp was visible beneath. She glanced at Lucette, who was being led by her mother, and dipped her head in a slight nod.

Lucette nodded back, even as her mother grasped her hand tighter and pulled her close. Farther down the hall, Mama Metcalf came out of one of the rooms, waved at her, then disappeared down an intersecting corridor.

This part of the hospice, which was where the sickest of the guests were put, felt different to everywhere else in the facility. There was little in the way of natural light, only the humming fluorescents, their glow reflected in the over-polished floor. Lucette found it odd that the shadows of the facility didn't bother her, whilst here in Corridor 3 it was the brightness that made her anxious. It smelled like the school lavatories after the janitor had been through—over-cleaned, artificial. Plus, on top of having to wear the stupid mask over her nose and mouth, this was the only place in the building, with the exception of the front door, that required a code to gain entry. Lucette didn't think her mother had realized she could see the numbers punched into the wall-mounted keypad outside.

67845 followed by the # key.

Lucette—who was repeating the entrance code over and over in her head—peaked into the rooms as they walked by, seeing other patients lying in bed or sitting up, some alone, some with family around them. At least each interior had a window, though there wasn't much sun anymore. The clouds had won the day.

She wasn't sure she could have explained it if asked, but being here in the hospice made her feel even more adult. This wasn't school with its silly games and boring lessons. This was a grown-up world full of grown-up problems. Despite the sadness that hung in the air, Lucette felt privileged to be here, leaving her to think that maybe getting older wasn't quite as bad as she'd assumed.

They stopped at an open door and her mother rapped on the jam.

"Come in," a soft voice said.

The first thing Lucette saw as they stepped into the room was the origami crane that she'd made for him sitting on the table by the bed. And then, of course, there was Robby reclined against the mattress. She knew he was about her age, though he looked like a little old man in a twelve-year-old's body. Except for his eyes. They sparkled just like hers.

"Hello there, I'm Robby." His nostrils were chapped and red, obvious that he'd been blowing and wiping his nose a lot.

At first there were no words. Her mother touched her shoulder again. A gentle squeeze. She hadn't realized how much she'd needed that affirmation until it was given. "Hi, I'm Lucette."

"So you're the one who made me the crane, huh?"

"Yeah. I know it's not the best."

"I think it's great. Maybe you could teach me how you do it."

"Sure. I'm working on another one right now. Cranes are the hardest origami to do."

"What's the easiest?"

"Probably a bat."

"Will you show me?"

Lucette looked up at her mother. Emily nodded and let her go. Lucette walked over to the bed and climbed into the chair beside it, slipping off her backpack and digging through it as she went. "A bat should really be done with black paper. I've only got white."

"It'll be an albino," Robby said with a laugh, and for a moment he didn't look quite so old.

Lucette took it nice and slow, explaining each fold as she went, repeating certain memorized passages from her book word for word. Five minutes later, she had a decent looking bat, and even demonstrated how you could make the wings flap by squeezing the middle section.

"That's cool, Lucette. You think you could teach me?"

"Sure thing. Right now I'm trying to figure out how to get that crane right. Maybe we can work on it together."

"That sounds great," Emily said, startling Lucette, who had almost forgotten her mother was in the room. "But it'll have to be another time. Robby needs his rest, and we need to go."

"Come on, Mom, just a little bit longer."

"I have to stop by the grocery store on the way home, my shift's over, and now it's time to say your goodbyes."

"Can she visit me for longer tomorrow?" Robby asked. "I'd like to learn how to do this origami stuff. It gets real boring here by myself."

Lucette turned to her mother and gave her a pleading look.

"Fine. How about tomorrow I bring Lucette over right after lunch and you can spend the afternoon visiting."

"Awesome," Lucette said. She knew tonight she'd have to endure another of her mother's extended lectures about rules, do's and don'ts, and appropriate behavior, but endure it she would. She craved companionship every bit as much as the sick boy on the bed.

"I'll see you tomorrow, Robby," she said, placing the albino bat on the table next to the malformed crane.

"I can't wait."

Taking her mother's hand, they stepped back out into the hallway where Mama Metcalf was waiting for them. "Heading out?" the old woman asked them.

"Yeah, we are. I just introduced Lucette to Robby."

"Did you just? Oh, that's a fine idea. There's no better medicine than a friend."

In the harsh Corridor 3 light, Mama Metcalf managed to look even older. Every wrinkle of her skin was illuminated. But that's what Lucette figured this part of the hospice was: A place of truths. The old woman struck her as tired looking, more tired, in fact, than she ever imagined someone could be without falling over. It occurred to Lucette then that the patients were not the only people within these walls in need of medicine.

Mama Metcalf took a step closer, almost excitedly; passing her weight from foot to foot in a manner that Lucette's mother would refer to as a mean case of 'ants in your pants'.

"I've been meaning to ask you something," she began. "What are you and the young'un doing Christmas night?"

***

Emily walked her daughter through the hospice in the direction of the front exit. Was she still angry? Yes. But the burn of that anger, at least, had dissipated. Rage could be a powerful thing. It encompassed all else, blinding her to where she wanted to be—on the other side of the moment, in a future where there was happiness. And Emily was almost there, thanks to three definite ticks in the pro column.

First:

Mama Metcalf had helped with her warm-hearted invitation to spend Christmas evening together at the older woman's house. Emily had accepted without missing a beat. This way, at least, they could be together.

There's no better medicine than a friend.
She hoped that was true.
Second:
Lucette had followed the rules, hadn't gotten into trouble, and as a reward, had been allowed to visit Robby. That meeting had also gone well. Better, perhaps, than Emily had expected it to. The boy was in Corridor 3 for a reason. It was where the dead went to die, though that wasn't to say humanity had to be checked at the door.
And third:
Emily's anger had been eroded by *pride*. Good old-fashioned chest-pumping pride. And not the kind evoked by movies either, or a damn fine novel; rather, the pride a mother feels for her child when she knows deep down in her bones that the right thing has been done, and that it was her own flesh and blood with the nerve to enact it. Nobody would deny that, by the book, Lucette *had* done wrong, but the reasoning behind her actions was commendable. Sometimes wrong was right—a fact that Emily couldn't voice to her child, not yet. Part of being a good parent was learning when to hold back how you felt, to censor when necessary, and to judge when honesty was appropriate. Lucette was growing up. When you stopped learning from your mistakes, you started to make your way down your own private Corridor 3.
Evolve or die. That's all there has ever been.
They were almost out of the building when Emily saw something that made her cold all over. She stopped, Lucette continuing on ahead before reaching the limitations of their interwoven hands.
"What is it, Mom?"

115

Lucette's question rung in her ears, echoing on and on, fading; the thrum of shoes dwarfed this sound. Three men and two women were being led toward them by Mrs. Woods. It was these visitors' inconspicuous clothes that gave them away, that and their matching stares—seemingly vacant, only not.

Woods led them by. Her boss didn't spare a glance for Emily, unlike her entourage. They trailed her face as they passed, their eyes twisting without moving their heads, like the glare of portraits in a gallery that you knew were watching, whilst not watching. A *nothing* that was a *something*.

The Crowners.

Emily watched them slip out of sight. She turned back to face the exit and ushered her daughter toward it. Not even gin would help her sleep that night.

***

Geraldine Leonard spared a thought for the nurse and the kid as she rounded a corner and shadowed the warden down an adjoining hall. This was no place for tots, and anyone who thought otherwise was a fool. But with desperation enough, anything was possible. This, Geraldine had seen more than once. No doubt the woman—likely a single mother—couldn't find a sitter or daycare willing to take her girl, and as a result, was forced to bring her to work. As to why she wasn't at school, well, that Geraldine didn't allow herself the effort of speculating. And of course the warden would have let the nurse do this; the warden may have done it herself over the years. And why?

Our capacity for desperation is one of the few things that binds us.

This facility was just the same as any other across

116

Chicago, across the whole Godless country. Whilst all around them society descended into over-regulated conservatism (cinema, television, the Internet, and literature taking the hardest prohibitive hits—people had actually been fined for reading banned 'supernatural' books and comics featuring the undead, even those published well before the outbreak), religion had taken an unexpected backseat.

Geraldine had been of the assumption that the apocalypse, which she'd always known would come on slow, would end up sending people flocking back to the church. Only no. Faith, itself, had been *infected*. Though in the end, at the pitiful, sad conclusion of it all, most people came around. Death made believers out of most.

And that was her role amongst the five; and there always were five.

One Ministry official, someone to ensure policy was enacted.

Three conscripted Ministry workers, drawn through an automated selection process, to serve as 'witnesses'. Geraldine had read that the firing squad consisted of people whose weapons were loaded with blanks—bar one gun. No members of the squad, who then fired in unison, would ever know whose bullet had ended the life. This helped assuage guilt. Being a witness was a political expression; those three were present to dilute the *responsibility*. It was a graceless, essential role.

Geraldine was pastoral care. Multi-faith, when she had to be.

The warden led them into their secured ward, what the five—and in all likelihood, the staff also (because why wouldn't they?)—referred to as 'death row'. A thing may have a name, but more often than not, peeling back the political correctness to reveal the nasty honesty beneath was healthier.

So this was death row. If the men and women within it avoided their intervention, well, then they would become zombies. Or bone eaters. Or smilers. And they, the five, were Crowners. That sounded a lot healthier than 'End of Life Policy Counselors', which was what it said on their tax returns.

They all had a job to do, one that Geraldine had been doing for too long. There had been a time, in Nicaragua as a missionary, when she thought she'd seen the worst this world had to offer. Today, like the day before that, would only prove how incorrect she was.

Bed C-2. Name: Mabry, Edward. That was what it said on the file. That was who they were here to 'counsel'.

The warden had the nurses in Corridor 3 close all of the doors to the rooms except 'Eddie's'. The man's next of kin, someone named Vick, stood nearby; he insisted on staying by Eddie's side until the very end. Personally, Geraldine disapproved of private citizens being present for the crowning, but they were allowed as long as the patient had given prior written consent, which Eddie had done.

Granted privacy in the hall, the warden and two of the witnesses flicked the brakes off the bed and wheeled it out through the wide-set architrave. Eddie was no longer attached to any floor-mounted apparatuses, just a cordless mobile syringe-driver the size of a deck of cards. Geraldine saw it now as they passed her by, latched to his bone-white arm, pumping the poor soul full of morphine.

Once you were hooked up to that device there was no going back.

The bed wheels squeaked, rattling off course like an out of control supermarket cart. Geraldine watched them wrestle with its weight, a small glimmer of humor in this otherwise humorless place.

They didn't speak, not conversationally, anyway. Why indulge in idle chitchat when there was nothing of worth to be said? That was her approach. Always had been. Most of the rules that got her through Central America in the 1980s still held true today, her ability to only use the words that counted being one of them.

And nothing mattered more than those slipping from her mouth now, as clattering yet whispery as the rosary beads beneath her layman's jacket, slightly muffled by the mask over the lower half of her face. "Our Father, who art in Heaven, hallowed be thy name."

Her prayer was the only sound, that and the screeching wheels, as they entered the security-locked antechamber at the end of Corridor 3. The wide windowless door opened to reveal the equally windowless room. As expected, or perhaps dreaded, the abattoir tiles had been recently cleaned for their arrival.

The warden flicked all four bed brakes with her heel and gave them a curt nod, which was all that was required. Geraldine admired the woman's efficiency, a trait that would see her go far in the pursuit for dignity. It was the sentimental that made the difficult jobs of this world hard to accomplish. And when it came to difficult vocations, being a Crowner was second only to the Cloth.

With the warden gone and the door locked, the five were ready to complete their work. They did so with an appropriate detachment, each of their movements syncopated and well-rehearsed, a ballet. The only music was Geraldine's recital of the Lord's word.

Vick took up position in the far corner of the room. Geraldine noted with approval that the man did not cry, merely stood rigidly and watched with an expression of stoic resolve.

The crown itself was kept in a Ministry-enforced, monitored, and maintained cabinet set into the wall. It was locked away, just as it should be, and was only accessible to those with a government-issued skeleton key. This added security measure made sense: only those with the appropriate authority to use the apparatus would ever need access it. Of this there were no variables. Or excuses.

They unlocked the cabinet and withdrew the crown, a heavy and industrial looking instrument that clashed with any notion of the modern world. It was something from a junkyard, a medieval throwback. It was, however, very effective.

Geraldine held the man's forearm. It was as cold as she expected it to be. His face had sucked back in on itself, as though there were a vacuum inside him. All of his hair had fallen out and his mouth was now set in the smiler's grin that lent the offensive term its name.

"Amen," she said, stepping back to let another one of the three witnesses—the rookie, Geraldine suspected, on account of the tears—place the crown over Eddie's head. She referred to him as this and not Edward because 'Eddie' was listed on his file as his preferred name.

In life, there was dignity in addressing peoples' predilections. There should be no difference in death. Anything less was a butchery.

And there was going to be butchery enough here.

The crown was called so on account of the six retractable bolts affixed to its metal headband. Geraldine watched the rookie place it around Eddie's temple. It was a one-size-fits-all apparatus, so little maneuvering was required. The five of them returned to the cabinet, faced it, and saw the five red switches along its lower sill.

Geraldine let her eyes drift shut, as she always did, and in the cloying quiet of the chamber listened to the man—who was loved, who was someone's son once, someone's employee, someone's hope—take his final breath. It hitched and gargled, evidence enough that the right decision had been made.

The government official set off the timer next to the crown's holster. A five second countdown clicked into life on a small screen. It used to be a ten seconds, but an operator survey from two years' before revealed that workers found that too long a time to wait. Five seconds of agonized patience was more than sufficient.

Five.

Behind Geraldine's eyes she could see the jungles of Nicaragua. The faces of the people she helped save. Broken faces, reset jaws. All smiling. A missing finger on a hand gripping the habit she used to wear back then.

Four.

The mosquito net she'd strung over her bed in her missionary villa. Stagnant air. Hundreds of blood-hungry insects trying to bite her through the thin cloth she'd patched with Band-Aids.

Three.

There was the husband she almost took before her calling. It had been at university in Idaho. His name had been Benjamin, and her parents found him a fine suitor. Geraldine could see his cleft lip now, etched against the black of her eyelids with the delicate definition of cracked tissue.

Two.

She forced it all away now, the descent of the mist. What prayers lingered were for the benefit of herself. They ran through her emptying head, light through the gloom.

One.

Nothingness. Fullness. Her throbbing pulse.

Zero.

They flicked the switches in unison, and as Geraldine did every time, jumped at the *hiss-thump* of the crown shooting its retractable prongs into Eddie's skull with quick, painless precision. She opened her eyes, knowing that the worst was not yet over, but too frightened by the nothingness in the dark. That, more than anything, terrified her.

She listened to the crown withdrawing its impalers, the tick-tocking of a backwards running watch. And then, the rain.

That was what she told herself. Only this rain was red. Soon the spurts subsided and the five braced themselves to turn, each unaware of who had dealt the deathblow, and hoping against hope that it had not been them.

Eddie gave a final kick. His arm dangled over the side of the rubber-covered hospital mattress. He was still now, as graceful in death as Geraldine hoped he had managed to be in life. Though of that, she wasn't the judge and jury. Yes, the world may be ending, but she still believed in some things.

The walls around the end of the bed, like the floor beneath those soon to squeak wheels, were adorned with ruby pinwheels of blood. It was an ugly, yet beautiful sight. Exquisite and pure.

Mercy was, in its own vile way, an act of art. And each time she was called up for crowner duty, she had no choice but to make each clemency a masterpiece. Such were the demands of her Calling.

Vick sobbed now, his stoicism abandoned. He crossed to Eddie's side and took the man's limp hand. Vick didn't even look at the Crowners, and they ignored his grief.

They left the room. Removing the bloodied crown, cleaning up the mess, and burning the body in the incinerator, was not within the parameters of their contracts. Those duties fell to the staff here at the hospice. Geraldine was confident this would be completed to perfection.

Cleanliness was next to Godliness. That's what her to-be suitor, Benjamin, used to say.

Before she killed him.

INTERLUDE FOUR

Turn the model over and repeat the prior instructions. When finished, fold the top wings into the center, doing the same action on the other side.

EMILY HAD ALWAYS known that there were places in this big ol' world where dark things grew. Nooks and crannies that safe people like her were privileged enough not to see. That privilege, of course, came from her self-proclaimed inclusion in the 'oh, it'll never happen to me' crowd, a special club that was nowhere near as exclusive as its members assumed, or hoped it to be. But the dark always ended up growing no matter where you went, even in the well-lit places. Such was the nature of shadows.

I thought we were safe.

Safe. Emily scoffed at the word now. Anyone who thought they were safe was deluded or over-faithed. Neither of which she found a suitable excuse anymore.

Because, yes. There *were* places where dark things grew, dark thoughts and acts and secrets and hatred. Only never once had Emily thought she'd live to see the day when such darkness would end up growing inside of her.

But then she would hear Jordan screaming in the

middle of the night and know that she was the same as everyone else. She was human, a pitiful creature plagued by the talents of hate and jealousy. Two emotions that she had mastered.

She ran to the spare room where he now slept. Still groggy with sleep, her hand brushed against the wall as she went, tilting framed photographs as she went. One crashed to the floor, tinkling glass.

Emily pushed the door open and flicked on the light. It smelled of sweat and urine in here. The overhead bulb burned bright, revealing her husband's skeletal frame on the mattress. He writhed, those whiter-by-the-day arms of his thumping the sheets.

These were the night terrors.

"Honey, honey," she said, crawling over to him and wrapping her arms about his shoulders. Her fingers brushed against the raw ridges of his wound, which would never heal. Not really.

Jordan snapped out of his dream, his high-pitched wailing cut short. Jarring silence filled the space. And then he softly said, "They're in here. With us."

Emily looked at him, aching. Held him tight.

Everything that made Jordan the man she married was fading by the day. If only memories could be bottled and used as medicine, Emily thought, then she could uncork one now—perhaps something from when they were first dating and making such extreme efforts to please one another—and let him have a whiff. It would clear the cataracts growing over what should be his bright eyes; bring color back to his cheeks.

Such remedies did not exist. And the more Emily lingered on it, the more she thought that memories would only make things worse. They were each spiders in interwoven webs of reminiscences, every sticky cord of their making kept them housed, but also strung off into the distance, tied at the other end to so many experiences and places that they had shared together.

That was how she learned the darkness was growing inside her.

The only way Emily was going to get through this was to cut each web, severing herself from everything that made them who they were as a couple. It was too painful, and too tempting, to pluck each web and listen to the sweet reverberations of their history.

Snip.

There went their wedding day.

Snip.

There went the first time they made love.

Snip.

There went the day she gave birth to Lucette, the way Jordan had held her hand throughout it all, his forehead pressed against hers, just as it was now.

It wouldn't be long and he would turn, and the only sticky strands remaining would have to be severed, too. Then, and only then, would she let him fall into whatever lay below. This, she knew, would be the great agony of her existence. And the temptation to fling herself down after him was so very, very strong.

Such a thing was not an option. Lucette deserved better.

Jordan began to cry, tried to tell her how sorry he was, apologizing for every wrong thing he'd ever done, only his ability to articulate his words was growing more problematic by the day. His lips were beginning to withdraw.

Emily shushed him and ran her fingers through his

hair. Clumps of his once wavy locks came free of his scalp and stuck to the sweaty mattress. There had been a time when she had thought him so dashing—such an old fashioned word, yet appropriate—because of his hair, which he'd always been so fearful of losing.

"My dad was bald as a badger," he used to say as they both prepped themselves of a morning, sharing the same mirror. She would look at him, toothbrush tucked inside her cheek, and shake her head.

Even his vanity turned her on.

Snip.

Emily was downtown at the pharmacy pushing Lucette in her stroller when Sally, the mother of the child they had been planning to visit for his birthday on the day Jordan was infected, came up to her from between two aisles and forced her into an almighty hug. Sally and her husband Conrad were old college friends of her husband, but over the past few years, Emily had forged a relationship with them, even though their company was tiresome and strained. They didn't have much in common except kids of similar ages. Despite this, being held that way in the pharmacy, surrounded by shoppers she'd never met, with that shitty music playing from hidden speakers, Emily struggled to keep herself from screaming relief. Maybe she wasn't as alone as she felt.

"Jesus H. Christ, girl," Sally said, drawing back. "You're nothing but skin and bones!"

"I've been sick. And on the back of that I've been trying to shed a couple of pounds. You know how I always struggled to lose that baby weight? Now I have."

Emily's smile was as phony as a two-dollar bill, and just about as useful.

Sally kneeled in front of Lucette, who was only half awake, and ruffled her hair, pinched her cheeks. "Aren't you just cute enough to eat! And look at those shoes you got on. You're going to grow up to be a stunner, little one."

Lucette smiled, swung her feet back and forth, but didn't say anything in the way of reply. Emily had noted a distinct lack of words coming from her daughter of late, an observation that made her feel ill. Quiet trauma was often the worst, or so Emily had read.

Sally drew herself upright and narrowed her glare. "Are you sure you're okay, Em? I hope you don't mind me saying, but you look *tired*." Sally studied her as though she were an insect under a magnifying glass, something to be burned alive and pulled apart out of the cold-hearted curiosity of someone else's pain. "Actually, scratch that. Tired's an understatement."

"Yeah, I'm sure. All is well, as they say."

"Have you seen a doctor? I've got a good one. Let me give you her number."

"Oh, of course I've seen someone. I'll tell you what though, antibiotics aren't as cheap as they used to be."

"Is anything, girl? Who you been seeing?"

"Doctor Sanderson."

"Never heard of him. I'm going to text you the number of a Doctor Sylvia Lee. She's a godsend, trust me. Promise me you'll call her. I'll send the details through to you once I'm back in the car. Conrad's back there keeping an eye on Kevin. They both want chocolate. You'd think they were related, or something!"

Sally giggled at her little joke. Such a happy, blissfully unaware person. Emily admired her situation so much that not punching her was a struggle.

"How's Jordan doing?" Sally asked. "We've missed you two. It's been months since the party and we haven't heard a peep from either one of you."

"Sally, I'm so sorry. This damn summer flu has ripped right through us, one by one."

"Not Jordan and Lucette, too? Girl, I'm fixing you up a batch of my famous chicken soup. Enough to last you through to winter."

"Oh, you don't have to do that, Sally."

"I know I don't have to, but you know I'm going to anyway." Sally pulled her handbag tight and crouched down to Lucette's level again. "Momma tells me you've been sick, sweetheart?"

Emily felt her pulse racing. She was sure that every vein in her body was rising up through her skin to spell out in twisted, vine-like words, everything that Emily was trying to keep hidden. At every turn there was a possible betrayal. Perhaps she would trip on one of her lies; perhaps someone could see that something was wrong despite her well-rehearsed grimaces. And most precarious of all was her daughter and her trained monkey deceits.

"You feeling okay, Lucette?" Sally asked, her hand resting on the girl's knee.

Emily wanted to hit her husband's friend across the back of the head, snatch the stroller by its handle, and wheel herself back to their secured compound—their medieval castle, as she'd come to think of it, where the darkness hadn't just grown but taken over, as insidious as a single drop of iodine in a tub of water, spreading out in delicate swirls, almost elegant, to encompass the entire tank. Only Emily did no such thing. She simply stared down at the crown of Sally's head, at the thin line of her hair part.

Lucette didn't answer, though there was half a smile. That, at least, was something.

Sally turned to face Emily, who averted those concerned eyes, which burned into her like the ends of cigarettes, sizzling through the veil that had always separated their worlds. Emily stepped back, taking the stroller with her.

The contents of the small pink carry cart strung over her forearm had been seen. Bandages, antiseptic, cotton swabs, saline solution, scissors, a new set of nail clippers—and not the cheap kind, either. These little trinkets rattled too loud as she turned away, bones at the bottom of a tub revealed to the world after all the deceits had been drained away.

The house was gloomy and quiet. There were no screams that night. Emily wandered from room to room, checking the locks, peering out through the front curtains at the tall front fence at the end of the driveway. A car passed by on the street, casting manic light refractions over the front lawn—for a single terrible moment turning all of the old trees into an army of undead beings frozen in lurching, contorted poses. As to whether or not these sentinels were keeping others out, or them in, was too difficult to tell.

She'd gone down to the hardware store the day before and bought a machete. It was under her bed now. Sleeping with it there—on those random hours when sleep was granted to her—made her feel more at ease. Emily hated that it had come to that. Every rustle in the bushes outside the spare room window was not the squirrel or possum that it no doubt was. No. It was another smiler digging under the fence, hungering for the bones beneath their flesh. She couldn't help but wonder, once all this was over, if there would ever be a moment of relief in her future, and if not, wondered if such a future was worth surviving for.

These thoughts, and others, were too easily assuaged by the cool edge of the machete's blade as she tossed and turned. That was why, at three in the morning, she'd roused herself and scurried from window to window seeking out intruders, to then attack, and cut up into pieces. It was better to night-dream of hurting others, those who deserved it, than dwell on hurting herself.

A noise behind her.

Emily spun. Jordan was easing himself into one of the living room chairs. Once the tide of shock began to withdraw, illuminating the broken debris of her love for this man, she crossed the room and snuggled in close to him. Jordan's arms wrapped around her; there was still some warmth there. Emily planted kisses on his cheek, which in the dim hardly felt like cheeks at all—rather something carven from stone, yet still capable of emotion. There were tears there. She wiped them away and ran her hands over the ridges of his ribcage.

They only had sorrys for each other now. There was no more talk of what would come, of the dreams they shared, just an endless string of apologies for every fight they had let themselves fall into the trap of indulging, every lie, every inappropriate aside they had ever imagined. This cleansed them in some strange way.

Another car passed, kicking the living room into a whirlpool of light and dark. She saw the tent in his pajama bottoms, and hungered for him. Jordan made no advance, even though they both wanted it. Emily had done her research—they both had, in fact—and infection could be transferred through unprotected sex. She had contemplated digging through their bedside table for a condom more than once, but thought against it. There was too much risk involved.

But she freed his cock all the same, held its girth in the palm of her hand. It gave her so much pleasure to give Jordan pleasure. When he moaned, she also moaned, and it was genuine. She covered his mouth with her spare hand as he came—just a small, hot ooze—so Lucette wouldn't hear.

Finished, she guided him back to bed and tucked him in. She hurried to the bathroom at the end of the hall and scoured her hands with soap, just in case.

Alone, in bed again, with only her undirected hatred for everything that wasn't this awful situation, Emily searched for sleep. It eluded her, the sly thing that it was. She reached over the side of the mattress and fingered the machete.

SUMMER

ROBBY'S HARDLY TOUCHED *his meatloaf,* Lucette thought, crunching up her empty bag of pretzels and tucking it into the pocket of her jeans. Her mother was always at her for doing this, tissues in particular, as her forgotten trash ended up going through the wash and soiling the load. Lucette retrieved the bag with a sigh and placed it on the tray table and pivoted across the bed. It was important that she made an effort to be on her best behavior. If she didn't, this solo visit with Robby would be her last.

"Not a fan?" she asked.

Robby shrugged his shoulders. "Dunno. I'm hungry, I guess, only nothing's appealing." He turned to the room's single window in the wall, like a framed painting of the landscape, a skinless world of snow-white bones. Perhaps it gave him comfort knowing there was a wider existence beyond this place.

Or maybe it's mocking him. Gosh, I hope not.

"Want to work on the crane?" Lucette asked in an attempt to puncture his sadness, to let in a little light.

At first he didn't answer, just continued staring out at the sky. Snowflakes speckled the glass, melting into droplets. Robby turned back to her. He seemed to be smiling, but then again, he always seemed to be smiling now. The stage was being set for the end.

"Sure."

Lucette pulled out the supplies from her backpack and scooted the chair closer to the bed so she could use it like a table. She placed a sheet of paper in front of her and another across Robby's lap, and then propped the book on origami at the foot of the bed, the diagram splayed.

"Okay," she said, taking the paper in her hands. "We start out folding a diagonal so it makes a triangle. Then unfold it again."

The corners of Robby's lips quivered, and she figured he was trying to frown. "What's the point of folding it if we're just going to unfold it again?"

Lucette giggled. "I know it sounds silly, but we'll need that crease later."

Following the next picture in the diagram, she folded the lower edges up to the crease so the paper resembled a kite. Before moving on, she glanced at Robby to make sure he was keeping up, only to discover he was still working on the first diagonal fold.

"I'm slow," he said.

"It's my fault, I shouldn't be going so fast."

Robby let the paper flop back open; it slid off his lap and fluttered to the ground. "I can't concentrate." A sliver of drool slipped from his mouth—escaped from him, sudden and unexpected—and he cleaned it away with a self-conscious swipe.

Lucette gathered up her paper and the book. "Must get pretty lonely here."

Robby studied the window once more, nodded. "My family always had a real Christmas tree, not one of those fake deals. It smelled like pine." His snowman eyes blinked. "Only I can't smell nothing no more. And there's no tree in here at all. All the ones outside are dead, too."

Lucette reached down and retrieved the paper that had fallen off the bed. She began folding it, not to make origami, just to give her hands something to do. "Are you cold?" she asked, watching him shiver.

"A little."

Lucette drew the secondary blanket, pooled at his feet, up to his waist and folded it over nice and neat, just as her mother did for her sometimes. He crossed his hands over the weave, the fingers bunched together and curled like crisscrossed crow's feet. Were he to sprout matching wings, long dark feathers blooming out of his back, only then would he be free of this awful place.

And I'd want you to take me with you.

They looked to the window. "Screw winter," Lucette said. "It's summertime."

"Ha. I wish."

"I'm serious. See the trees?"

"Uh-huh."

Lucette walked over to the glass separating in from out, warmth from imagined warmth, and put her finger to the scrim of condensation. She gave him a cheeky smile, and with a giggle, drew leaves in the fog, ornamenting the skeleton trees outside. "There. See. It's summer again."

Robby laughed. "We can drink lemonade!"

"Oh, totally. And it'd be homemade, none of that store bought yucky stuff."

"What does it smell like? Outside, I mean." He

closed his eyes, hands clenching the blanket, and inhaled. "I can't quite—"

"Cut grass," she said, watching him exhale as though with relief.

"Yeah. That's it. Cut grass."

"And honeysuckle. I love honeysuckle. There are birds, too."

"I can hear them now."

Lucette watched Robby's eyes leap and dart beneath his lids as though he were sleeping, which to some degree, he now was. And she, Lucette realized, was the one creating his dream. Her stomach fluttered like the butterflies that no doubt danced through the field where they sat, bathing in sunshine and—

"Eating," she said. "Lots of food. You laid out one of those checkered tablecloths. You know, like the ones they put in fancy restaurants."

"A summer picnic. Perfect. When I'm done I'm going to put on my hat and dig for dinosaur bones. I'll find a big old T-Rex and lay it out on the ground."

"And then it'll get dark and some fireflies will come along and sit in the skull. They'll light up its eyes so it looks alive again."

Lucette let them both fall into silence in which they listened to each other breathing, savoring the images they had conjured. But she could sense the light in the dinosaur skull beginning to dim, those eyes darkening as night fell to gobble them up.

"I think by the time this snow melts, I won't be here anymore," Robbie said.

"Are—are you scared?"

Robby hesitated, nodded. "There's so much I wanted to do."

Lucette put the book back on the bed. Instead of sharing summertime, all they could share was their sighs. "Well, one thing you can do is learn to make a paper crane. There are people who live to be a hundred who never get to do that."

"Yeah. I guess you're right."

"Let's give it another try?"

His smile was genuine, not just a grotesque facsimile. "Deal."

Lucette pulled out a fresh sheet for Robby and they started again, following along with the diagram, taking it slow. They didn't speak for a while, cocooned by the sounds of the facility—footsteps, a cough, the drip-drip-drip of her friend's IV.

"Am I the first infected person you've ever been around?" This question, like the descent of night in their fantasy, came without preamble. It had a ring of inevitability to it.

Lucette shook her head, focusing on the fold she was making.

"Who?"

After a brief hesitation, she answered. "My dad."

"I'm sorry. I had no idea. Was he in a place like this?"

Another shake of the head. "No."

"I guess in some ways he was lucky, getting to die in his own bed surrounded by his family."

(But would you mind if I asked Miss Natalia a question or two?)

"We don't have to talk about this."

"No, it's okay. Mom thinks I don't remember, only I do. My father getting bit is my first memory. And how Mom tried to explain it to me, tried to get me to understand the rules, but I still didn't get it. I tried. I forgot. The rules, I mean."

"I get it, Lucette," he said, gripping her hand. "Trust me."

The conversation petered out, and the quiet became cottony, soft and gentle and soporific. As they contorted paper into intricate shapes, sometimes stumbling upon success and sometimes not, Lucette wondered what Robby was feeling, wondered if their summertime picnic was haunting him as it was her. Tablecloths and dinosaur bones, fireflies in twilight. And there, in the dark that always came, all of the things that Robby would never get to do.

Going places.

Doing things.

Becoming something.

Kissing a girl.

Lucette glanced down at her origami. The next one would be better—it had to be. She crunched it up and threw it at the wastebasket against the wall under the window. Missed. The leaves she'd drawn into life against the glass bled dewy threads extending down to the sill, and she watched, saddened, as it all faded away.

THE LAST CHRISTMAS

"**M**ERRY CHRISTMAS, Happy Holidays, Ho Ho Ho, and all that kind of bizzo!" Mama Metcalf said, opening the door. She wore a knit red sweater with a green Christmas tree stenciled across the front, actual silver bells dangling from it, and a Santa hat was perched on her head. Seeing this, Emily bleated, glad that she hadn't cancelled as she'd been tempted to.

"Good, lord! The same to you. You look quite festive."

"Well, way I figure it I only get to wear this stuff once a year. Might as well enjoy it."

"You've got a point there."

The house was small, a 'cracker box' as Emily's parents used to describe such homes, but it was warm—perhaps a little too warm even. Feeling as though she'd just stepped into an oven, Emily began to de-mummify herself from her layers of scarves and jackets, urging Lucette to do the same.

"Welcome to the Winter Wonderland," Mama Metcalf said as she took their gear and hung it by the front door.

It looked like a Christmas suicide bomber had come into the living room, yanked the ACME-style trigger, and exploded. Yes, as expected, there was the crackling fire, the massive tree dominating the far corner; but every square inch of space was packed with shrapnel from the blast. Knickknacks jostled for room on the mantle, toy elves poked out of stockings, Santa sentinels lined the windows, miss-matched nativity sets were perched on stools, with Joseph towering over Mary, a gargantuan baby Jesus larger than all three Wise Men combined. The coffee table was piled with plastic snowmen, ceramic Christmas trees, music boxes with glass ice skaters gliding across mirrored ponds, snow globes, and tinsel-haloed angels. From a small tape deck—Emily hadn't seen one of those in ages—Jim Nabors crooned Christmas classics, only there was no room left to roast those chestnuts over the open fire.

"No doubt what day it is when you come in my house," Mama Metcalf said. Her cheeks had a natural flush. Emily wondered if the old woman had been dipping into some spiked eggnog, and if so, for the love of all things holy, when would she please share.

"We brought you a present," Lucette said, holding the gift out. The wrapping was sloppy with excessive mounds of tape holding the edges down, but Lucette had insisted on wrapping it herself.

"Thanks so much. You go put that under the tree. I got presents for you too but we'll wait 'til after supper to open them."

Lucette ran to the tree, placing their gift down next to several others. "Mom, these are all for us."

"Mama Metcalf, you shouldn't have. That's way too extravagant."

"Oh, nonsense," the old woman said with a

dismissive wave of her hand. "I don't have any grand-young'uns, I gotta do something with my money."

Emily found herself staring at a photo hanging on the wall above the mantel, a somewhat younger Mama Metcalf posing with a handsome man with dark hair and a thousand-watt smile. "Is this your son?"

"Yup, that's my Erik when he was a senior in college. Ain't he a looker?"

"He has your eyes."

"He favors his Daddy more in the looks department. Luckily he got my temperament."

"Will your son be coming over tonight?" Lucette asked. The girl was wearing a green dress that Emily had gotten from a secondhand store with matching ribbons holding her hair in pigtails.

"No honey, Erik and his hubby were here last night for Christmas Eve. They spend Christmas night with Paul's family."

Emily remembered the pumpkin pie in her hands. "Where should I put this?"

"Follow me."

An archway led from the living room into a cramped, yet tidy kitchen. The invasion of holiday ornamentation hadn't spread this far except for a Santa and Mrs. Claus salt and pepper set on the table. The walls were a muted yellow, the appliances old but clean, and an enticing aroma of meat and spices thickened the air. Emily started to salivate, her stomach grumbling with anticipation.

"Just put the pie on the table there. I got turkey and ham, some dressing and cranberry sauce, macaroni pie and mashed potatoes, some deviled eggs, and green bean casserole."

"You really shouldn't have gone to this much trouble."

"Hush up, let an old woman have her fun. Everything should be ready in about fifteen minutes. Want a drink while we wait. Something warm?"

"That would be lovely."

Mama Metcalf whipped up two cups of instant coffee for Emily and herself, and some hot chocolate with extra marshmallows for Lucette. They sat at the table, sipping their steaming brews.

"I can't imagine all the grocery shopping you had to do for this meal," Emily said, hiding the grimace at the bitter taste of the coffee. She hated instant, but she was a guest and didn't want to be rude.

Mama Metcalf laughed. "Was a haul, that's for sure, and I had an interesting encounter in the parking lot."

"What's that?"

"Well, I ain't got no car so I took a cab to and from the grocery store, and the cab driver wouldn't help me load the groceries into the trunk, said it wasn't part of his job, but then this man came up and asked if I needed some assistance. He was an old coot, looked like maybe he was a boy when Washington chopped down that cherry tree, but I was glad of the help. He was certainly the chatty type, but that ain't never bothered me none. When all the groceries was packed away in the trunk, he offered to take the cart back for me, and then he asked if he could have my number."

"Your number?" Emily said with a smile. "Mama Metcalf, were you getting picked up in a parking lot?"

"I don't know why I gave it to him. He was just being so nice, I figured what the hay."

"Did he call?"

Mama Metcalf nodded. "This morning. Was telling me how his kids and grandkids was gonna be coming over tonight from all over the country. Was having a nice little talk 'til he started saying all this stuff about wanting to get me under the mistletoe. I had to stop him right then and there, told him, 'Mister, that is *not* gonna happen!'"

Emily burst into laughter, even as she glanced over at Lucette, worried the conversation might be taking too adult a turn, but the little girl was engrossed with the salt and pepper shakers, which she was making dance across the table. Her daughter was no doubt playing possum though; she heard, she understood.

"You don't ever want a little companionship?" Emily asked in a confidential voice that she hadn't heard herself use since back when she had girlfriends and went to baby showers and played Bridge on Wednesdays. Memories of someone else's life— someone naïve, blind.

"Not like that, no thank you. I ain't got no use for romance in my life, not at my age."

Emily stared into her murky coffee. Here she was counseling Mama Metcalf about male companionship when Emily herself had more or less lived like a nun since Jordan died. Sure, there had been a few failed dates, a couple of half-hearted 'not so loud, you'll wake my girl,' fumblings in the dark. Nothing lasted, of course; men had a way of sniffing out trauma, it clung to some women like the stink of smoke. Emily knew she was one such person. Occasional pings rung through her newfound asexuality, but she didn't follow through on the urge. Even simple old-fashioned fucking took time, and what little time she had was consumed by motherhood—the emergencies, the pandering, the tests, the fights, the hugs, the kisses, the lessons, the elastic limits of tolerance.

Love had to take the backseat, a bitter irony if there ever was one.

Loud gurgling pulled Emily from her reverie, and she turned to Lucette. The girl clutched her stomach, a blush creeping into her cheeks. "Sorry, everything just smells so good."

"Well," Mama Metcalf said, pushing against the table as she got to her feet, "I'd say supper is just about ready."

***

Emily and Lucette—darlings that they were—told her how delicious everything was, but Mama Metcalf thought the turkey was too dry and the potatoes too lumpy. Something was off about the deviled eggs as well, maybe not enough mayo. Still, it was nice to be sharing food with people she liked. Not that she hadn't enjoyed the meal with her son and his husband the previous evening, but Erik and Paul were both vegetarians and had brought over something called 'tofurkey', which tasted like boiled tires, or so she imagined.

"I like your sweater, Mama Metcalf," Lucette said, nibbling on a slice of ham.

"Thank you, honey. My Erik gave this to me last Christmas."

"What did he get you this year?" Emily asked.

Mama Metcalf reached up to either side of her head, tapping the dangling silver reindeer that hung from her earlobes.

"Lovely," Emily said.

"You're like a walking Christmas tree," Lucette chimed in.

"I guess I am that."

Lucette leaned forward and said in a stage-whisper, "I didn't get Mom anything. We were going to make a Christmas wreath in school, then I stopped going."

Mama Metcalf mimicked the girl's posture and whisper. "Don't worry about that. What young-uns don't get is their very existence is a gift to their parents."

Emily reached out to stroke one of her daughter's pigtails. "I hope Lucette and I are always as close as you and Erik."

Mama Metcalf nodded, returning to her dinner. She recalled playing dress up with Erik when he was three or four, him scooting around in her high heels (always when his father wasn't home); evenings spent watching *Steel Magnolias* or *Golden Girls* reruns together. When Erik came out of the closet, his father blamed her for turning their son into a sissy, though she knew better. It was the way he had been born, like some people having blue eyes and others green. It was merely different, neither better nor worse.

Over the years, that closeness waned. Once he went off to college and moved from South Carolina, she saw him just on holidays and not even all of them. Phone calls became infrequent. Erik was always after her to get an email account, only she didn't trust computers. She wouldn't even have a cell phone if he hadn't bought one for her.

She thought moving to Chicago would bridge the

emotional distance between them by bridging the physical. Things hadn't worked out that way. If she was lucky, she saw Erik once every few months, and phone calls were still few and far between, and she was usually the one doing the dialing. Yes, he was a busy man, but she'd uprooted her life and moved to an unfamiliar place where she knew no one just to be nearer to him. The least he could do was make time for his poor old Mama. After all, she wasn't going to be around forever.

One of the main reasons she'd decided to start volunteering at the hospice was to get out of the house. Loneliness drove her to it, the same loneliness that had caused her to give her number to the old coot in the grocery store parking lot. She hadn't been lying to Emily earlier; she had no desire for romance at this point in her life, although the idea of someone to call and talk to was not without appeal.

You got a new friend sitting right across the table from you, she reminded herself. *So stop wallowing in self-pity and be a good guest like your Mama taught you.*

"Got any big plans for New Year's Eve?" she asked Emily.

"I'm working the morning shift. After that, well, probably the same thing I did last year. Have a quiet dinner with Lucette then turn in early. I'm on leave after that for a bit."

"I wanna stay up and watch the ball drop," Lucette said. "Mom won't let me."

Emily gave the girl a stern look. "The year will switch over whether or not you're awake to see it, young lady."

"You know, I can always watch the young'un that night if you want to go out."

"That's very nice of you. It's unnecessary though."

"I hear the riverfront is quite the scene on New Year's Eve. Of course, I'm too old for that kind of thing myself, but a young thang like you should be out and about mingling."

"I'm not terribly social."

"Sounds like prime resolution material to me."

"Hey, I'm here tonight, aren't I? I call that a first step."

"I reckon you're right, but steps eventually need to turn into leaps if you're gonna get anywhere."

"You know the old expression about looking before you leap?"

"How about this? You and the young'un come spend New Year's Eve with me. I'll make a big bowl of popcorn and we'll let Lucette have her first ball-drop experience."

Lucette, who had been staring off through the archway at the Christmas tree, specifically at the presents under its branches, turned back. "Can we, Mom? Please?"

"I'll think about it," Emily said.

The little girl clapped, and truthfully Mama Metcalf felt like joining her. No one should be alone on New Year's.

You thinking about Emily and Lucette, or yourself, ol' girl?

It didn't matter either way, she figured.

With the main meal finished, they armed themselves

with a wedge of pie apiece and ambled back into the living room. The Christmas tree towered over them, a totem to less desperate times. Lucette dropped to her knees and reached for a present. "Darlin', I think we should let Mama Metcalf go first," Emily said. "It's her house, after all."

Lucette stared at the gifts with her name on them—so close and yet so far—but didn't muster an ounce of protest. This warmed Mama Metcalf. The girl had fine manners, a trait as rare as hen's teeth in this day and age. Lucette handed her a present, which she unwrapped, revealing a glass jewelry box with a plush red interior.

"Oh, it's beautiful. I love it."

"Now you have somewhere to put your reindeer earrings," Lucette said.

"That I do, honey. Now why don't you open that big one with the red wrapping?"

Lucette looked to her mother first, and when Emily nodded, the girl grabbed the gift.

"What did you get from—" Mama Metcalf almost said *Santa Claus*, but remembered the girl knew certain things about life that other girls her age did not. "—your mom?"

"She got me this big book on origami so I don't have to keep renewing the one from the library. And a baseball bat—*can you believe it!* So cool. Oh, and clothes."

"You needed those clothes," Emily said, measured, defensive. Mama Metcalf had also picked up on Lucette's dismissive tone in regards to her essentials, but only smiled. She'd been the same when she was young, rifling through presents as the snow fell outside, shaking boxes for the gold whilst leaving the soft packages until last.

Lucette unwrapped the gift, and her eyes widened. "Oh, thank you, Mama Metcalf!"

She held a large dollhouse with peekaboo doors and multiple rooms, a curving flight of stairs, tiny furnishings. There was even a perfect-looking plastic family within its walls—a mother, father, child, faces molded into never-ending grins.

***

Emily sipped from her cup, the spiced eggnog tickling her in all the right ways, and looked at the wrapper wreckage at their feet. Mama Metcalf had given them half a dozen presents each. Some of them were *interesting*, to say the least, like the decorative plate that depicted the birth of Hiawatha, for example. Regardless, the woman's generosity was touching.

They stayed until half past nine, then gathered up their bounty, put on their coats, and got ready to head out into the cold. Lucette was more tired than she was letting on. It had been a big day, though not half as harrowing as the Christmases leading up to it. Anniversaries, birthdays, holidays—each flick of their paper calendar pages cut like a razor when the one person you longed to share them with was dead. 'They' said time healed all wounds when in fact it only numbed the creeping spread of gangrene. It saddened Emily to think how grateful she was for even this minor reprieve.

At the doorway, Mama Metcalf touched her shoulder and said, "You know, about a year ago I thought I had flesh-eating virus on my face."

Emily had gotten used to the woman's out of the

blue non-sequesters, but this was particularly bizarre and actually stunned her silent for a moment. "Um, excuse me?"

"Yeah, I got these blisters and rash on the side of my face, on my left cheek and down under my chin. I wasn't sure what it was, but then I saw this news story about an outbreak of flesh-eating virus in Africa or somewhere like that. I started to worry that I'd got it, so I went to see my doctor. Turned out it was just a case of the shingles."

Biting her bottom lip to keep from laughing, Emily strained to understand what this story had to do with anything. "Well, I'm glad it turned out not to be anything serious."

"Exactly," Mama Metcalf said in a triumphant tone that suggested the meaning of the story should now be clear. "Sometimes we think something is going to be the death of us, only it turns out to be something that hurts for a while and eventually fades."

Now Emily saw what the old woman was getting at, and she felt heat suffusing her cheeks and stared down at her shoes.

Mama Metcalf touched her shoulder again. "I ain't asking no questions because it ain't my business, but it's obvious you got something in your past that still haunts you and you carry a sadness with you wherever you go. I'm just saying that you should remember that sometimes what seems like a flesh-eating virus turns out to only be a case of the shingles."

"Thank you," Emily mumbled. "I mean, for everything."

"Wasn't nothing. Remember, you and the young'un promised to come visit with me on New Year's."

"Yes please," Lucette said, swinging the plastic grocery bag full of her gifts.

Emily looked up to meet Mama Metcalf's eyes. "Definitely."

On the drive home, taking it extra slow on the icy roads, Emily thought about what the old woman had told her. Mama Metcalf meant well with her homespun advice, but she didn't know Emily's secrets.

Sometimes the rash turned out to be flesh-eating virus after all. And the wound was growing more septic by the day.

THE UGLIES

THE FIRST TIME Robby experienced a night terror, back in the early days of his infection, he had no idea what was going on. Something bitter twinkled to life in his dream, twisting the otherwise innocuous imagery into a nightmare that didn't end with waking. This was always the worst part. The leftovers. Whatever despicable things the fever conjured in the dream—the uglies, as he'd come to think of them—followed him into reality. There they would linger.

The uglies were with him that Christmas night. They stood at the foot of his bed.

He'd gone to sleep thinking about the summer Lucette had whispered to life earlier that week. The checkered cloth across the grass, the leaves on the tree, fireflies in the eyes of the dinosaur skull. But his fatigue had been deep. His limbs had grown heavy, as though he weren't dressed in a gown but an iron suit, like the kind deep-sea divers wore in old movies. And then the heaviness dragged him into the dark where he was alone for a while. Schools of half-memories—fickle and quick as fish—had swished about him. He tried to reach out and grab one, to savor the good times. They were too fast.

But then the uglies had come.

It was a terrible feeling. He wanted to wake up, only he knew that being awake was *worse* than the nightmare. The dream, at least, was numb. No pain. Were he to wake, not only would the uglies be there but there would be the gut-wrenching agony of the fever, too.

No escape.

Robby bolted upright in bed, thrashed against the mattress, yanking the IV cord from his arm. A patter of saline across the linoleum. It was pitch black. The night wasn't done with him yet.

It came at him then, the aches seizing his body. He saw color when he blinked, starbursts of pain. Sweat coursed down his face. It was so damn hot. Robby wouldn't have been at all surprised if the walls started to blister and his skin bake. The uglies brought invisible fire with them each and every time.

He blindly reached for his emergency buzzer. It wisped off the hospital bed. Fighting through pain— God how his joints screeched when he moved—Robby tried to find it in the dark. Dizziness sent everything into a spin, and for a moment he was worried he might vomit, or 'blow chunks' as he and the other boys at school used to say. This expression he'd learned the day he'd vomited at assembly in the fourth grade, struck down with heatstroke at the peak of July's heat. Unlike that one embarrassing time, with the teachers swarming over him as the kids laughed and pointed, he didn't blow chunks now. But he did tumble free of the sheets and thump to the floor.

Robby hugged his chest, imagining that his arms were not his own but belonged to his mother. He could feel his ribs through the gown, shocking his wishes away. This couldn't be his body. Surely not. In his head he still had a bit of puppy fat on him. Also in his head he was dressed in his father's I'VE GOT MOXIE cap; his skin was blemished with scraped knees from coming off his bike, from the occasional schoolyard scuff—not from bedsores and trails of IV puncture marks.

In his head, Robby was happy. Loved.

In the real world though, here within the hospice, he was neither. Sure, he had a couple of friends, that Lucette with her pretty pigtails and old Mama Metcalf who smelled like mothballs and grandmotherly perfume, the friendly social workers and the psych. But they weren't the one person he needed right now. They weren't his mother, the woman who said she loved him. Once upon a time. Dad, less so. Robby remembered the way his father had snatched the Moxie cap off his head and how it had made him feel.

The school of memories swished by. Close enough to catch glimmers within the bubble.

Mom's smile as she picked him up from school.

Savory, sweet—the flavors of her homemade pasta sauce.

The way he could smell her when she left the room. For a while, at least.

Gone. Vanished. And in their place there was only the darkness of the room he would no doubt die in, and soon.

It was such a strange thought. That he wouldn't exist. He wondered if being pulled from this world and into whatever came next hurt, or would it be like waking from one of his nightmares? Would he bolt awake in the Heaven he'd heard so much about? What if there was nothing over there? Robby wasn't sure which concept frightened him more.

Or maybe I'll become a ghost. If so, I'll haunt Lucette to keep her company, just as she haunts me here. I'll be a friendly ghost, a regular Casper. I won't rattle chains. I'll play tricks on her. I'll knock the Fruit Loops *off her spoon when she sits down to have breakfast in the morning. I'll draw shapes in the frost of her window, smiley faces, leaves. This will be my thank you.*

But until that time arrived he had this world to deal with, every slow and painful second of it.

Robby rolled onto his side and felt around for the buzzer. Found it. Pressed the trigger. He heard the faint chime of the display board outside his door. Hopefully someone would come. They often didn't.

Especially at night.

He wasn't alone. The uglies were under the bed with him.

Their white faces stared at him, all rising in unison to smile. Rat teeth. Their eyes were so black, as though they had drawn all the ink out of the shadows.

Robby backed out from under the bed and saw more uglies crawling all over the room, across the walls, defying gravity to skirt the ceiling. They were naked. Men, women, children. A shifting, writhing tapestry of flesh in the moonlight squeezing through the window.

One dropped to the ground and came at him. It was the man who had taken him at the fair. Long fingers, the nails sharp and dirty, stretched towards him. Robby unlocked the scream that he'd been keeping in his throat. It echoed in this cell, louder than the hisses and grunts of the uglies as they bit and chewed at each other, animals fighting for ownership over his bones.

Robby had never hated anything in his life. Not really. Just superficial stuff. Sure, there had been bullies at school, food that left a bad taste in his mouth. Nothing *pure*. That was until the hatred he felt for the *thing* that had touched him.

The mocking sound of safety up the ravine.

And like true hatred, Robby hadn't known what true terror was, either. That, too, changed Halloween night, there in the ravine with the leaves in his mouth, blood coursing down his chin from where he'd bitten his lips.

That man was back now to make Robby one of his own. One of the uglies.

Robby buried his head in the crook of his arm, screaming, crying. He pressed the trigger on his emergency buzzer again, the electric cord wrapped around him.

Hot breath on his neck.

(this can't be happening)

The jingle-jangle of a distant carousel. Pain.

(I'm too young to die)

He listened to the uglies scratch down off the walls and come after him. Pale blurs in the dim, as though they burned with their own inner light, their own personal fevers, illness that drove them to terrible and violent ends. Robby wondered who each of them had been before they 'turned', wondered who their mothers were, and if they were still loved in ways that he no longer was or ever would be again.

This isn't how things were supposed to happen.
I was supposed to be me.
Not this.

Robby tried to scramble away, knocking the bedside table and sending plastic cups and forks in every direction. Something brushed against his face. Maybe one of his or Lucette's origami attempts. The uglies skittered about him, hot as flame, boiling his blood. He smelled shit and piss in the stagnant room. His own.

Robby was too weak to get to his feet. He lifted his head and saw the window on the opposite side of the room; it had never seemed so small. It shrunk down to a pinpoint as he tumbled onto his back again, revealing the ceiling where another ugly was poised, arching its spine to reveal its hairless face, the bone-eating grin. Robby bellowed again, louder than before, when he saw that the ugly above him was none other than himself.

It hissed, ready to leap.

And then the door to the room opened and one of the night nurses slammed on the lights. It was blinding. After a few moments Robby's eyes adjusted to the glare. It was just he and the man named Mykel there in the death room. The uglies may have vanished, but they had left him feeling burnt, broken. Spent.

***

Now that Mykel had settled the kid with a healthy dose of pandering and sedatives, he leaned against the FSU wall and rubbed his face through his mask. Night shifts were a bitch, and this was why. He put the shit and urine stained towels into a drawstring bag and dumped it in a trolley in the sluice room. A flick of the wrist and his rubber gloves were gone too, and he scrubbed his hands at the water station. "Happy fucking Christmas."

Another buzzer went off to his right, back down closer to the entrance/exit door. Still within FSU. It was the resident they all knew as Speedy.

Oh, come on. What now?

Mykel swanned into the room and found Speedy propped up against his pillow, the trigger of his emergency call still in his hand. As irritated as he was, Mykel had to admit a grudging respect for the man; he was tough. Speedy had been infected longer than anyone in the hospice and had been on the Final Stages Unit much longer than Robby. It might have been inspirational if it wasn't so futile and pathetic. The old man was lingering in a way no man really should.

Sometimes you just got to give up and let go.

Mykel shuffled over to the bed in the dark. Doing so, his thoughts turned to his parents and his younger brother Jeremy. This shouldn't have caught him off guard, but it did. His brother was a perfect example of someone, who like old Speedy, didn't know when to give up the ghost.

Jeremy had always been the golden child. Muscular, athletic, straight, a track star in high school, married the perfect young lady from a well-to-do-family. He had the Midas touch and could do no wrong. Unlike Mykel, the quintessential black sheep.

And yet Mykel hadn't been the one dumb enough to get bit by a bone-eater. No, that was perfect Jeremy with his good Samaritan routine. Driving home from the gym after nightfall, pulling over to help some old lady wandering down the centerline of the road in her nightgown. Even though it was the early days of the outbreak, it had still been stupid of Jeremy to compromise himself like that. The world had changed and his brother had been rewarded for his kindness with a single snap to his forearm.

"We'd prepared ourselves, deep down, to maybe lose you, Mykel," his father had confessed one night. A fair amount of imported beer already consumed, the bottle overturned between them, dripping onto the kitchen table they had shared so many dinners at. "You know, to AIDS or something. But not this. Not Jeremy."

That was the first and only time Mykel told his father to fuck off. His promise to never do so again was written in bruises.

Just let go.

Feigning that things were going to be okay was unhealthy. Sometimes you had to walk away from something good, sometimes you had to hurt the ones you loved. Pretending didn't help anyone. As far as Mykel was concerned, the moment you were bitten you were as good as dead. A walking corpse. And that was how Mykel managed to detach himself from the insanity of his job; his guests weren't people. They were things.

And the thing on the bed turned toward Mykel, spoke. "Is the boy all right?"

"For now, Speedy."

"I heard him screamin'. Is that what I sound like when the fever takes me?"

"Look, what is it I can help you with? I'm a busy man."

Speedy grabbed Mykel's forearm. "I can hear Tammy crying through the wall. I want to go see her."

"What?" It took Mykel a moment to realize Speedy was talking about the bag of bones that he thought of as Skeletora, the one Mama Metcalf was always playing cards with. "Why?"

"We've been—" Speedy paused, his ashen tongue sneaking out to try to moisten his dry, cracked lips. Each word came with great effort, exhausting him. "Close."

"Really?" Mykel said with a cocked eyebrow. So maybe the infected weren't *completely* dead after all, though how anyone in Speedy's condition could even think about things of a romantic nature was beyond him. If Mykel had the sniffles, he didn't want anyone to come within fifty yards of him. But Speedy was alone now, his wife having done what Mykel would have done, and let go. She hadn't been to see him in weeks, nor could he blame her. Infection killed the people you loved three times over. There was the initial bite and the way it severed all ties to the future you'd planned out for one other. There was the physical warping of the body as you watched everything that made someone identifiable as the person you committed yourself to rotted away, and then, after all this, there was the turning itself, the final nail in the coffin. Each phase tortured the surviving partner, forcing them into a self-preservation mode in which you either sunk or swam. The smart ones jumped ship and paddled for shore long before that, which is what Mykel had done, and if Jeremy begrudged him this from the grave, well, such was life. And death.

"It's just comfort," Speedy said. He was alert that

night, an unusual change from his drooling, incontinent self. Mykel thought about candles and about how they burned brightest just before they went out.

"I don't know if Woods would approve."

"Just half an hour. Help me walk in. I'm weak. She's scared. The little one's dying."

"Look, you should be resting."

"I'll rest when I'm dead, boy," Speedy said, letting go of Mykel's arm. "And you'll *rest* too someday. 'Til then, let us live. No woman should cry alone in the night, not on Christmas."

INTERLUDE FIVE

Fold both legs of the model upwards, crease with great pressure, and then unfold again. Inside reverse fold the legs along those creases you just made.

SALLY PARKED HER station wagon under an elm, its branches as old as any of the buildings in the city, its roots stretching back through layers of soil to a time when the ground was less bitter. Those days were gone, yet the determined though foolish tree lingered on. It offered shade to a world doomed to burn anyway, and not all the chicken soup in the universe would change that.

But regardless, she had to try.

The contents of the Tupperware container tucked under her arm sloshed as Sally made her way up the street in the direction of Emily and Jordan's house. A corridor of hedges zoomed by on her right, dead leaves crunching under her sneakers. The seasons had already started to mingle, a chill encroaching like an anti-fever.

It was just after ten in the morning and she'd left Kevin in her husband's care. Conrad was just as much a sucker for Saturday morning cartoons as their son. It made her happy to see the two of them entangled on the couch together in the living room, each donning matching milk moustaches. The boys were her everything, and she had no idea what life would be like without them. Hell, she didn't even like to think about it.

Sally reached Emily's familiar gated fence and slipped her sunglasses up onto the crown of her head to better see the shade-speckled front yard and driveway. Her heart was racing. Screw the double-shot latte she'd devoured earlier whilst sitting on the couch with her laptop across her knees, speculation was the ultimate stimulant. The headlines from the articles she'd been reading online still echoed through her head:

10 SIGNS SOMEONE YOU KNOW MAY BE INFECTED.
YOUR CIVIC DUTY: THE HARD CALL WE ALL MUST MAKE.
BONE EATERS MUST BITE THE DUST—A CALL FOR SURVIVAL.

Bandages. Antiseptic. Cotton swabs. Saline. Scissors. Nail clippers. All of this Sally had seen in Emily's basket at the pharmacy—items that appeared innocent enough, yet when viewed as a whole were rather telling. Especially when one other factor was considered: Jordan's absence. This was the primary fuel to her suspicion. It tickled her guts, shooed sleep away. Even Conrad, as blissfully unaware as he could be, had noticed that his friend wasn't contacting him for their once a month bar-hop, all of those unanswered emails and text messages.

I'm not going crazy. I know it.

Sally had asked herself multiple times where the

seeds of her motivation lay. Was attempting to visit Emily just about her frantic need to involve herself in the business of others, a flaw that had been pointed out to her so many times by former friends? Or was her disquiet genuine? This see-saw of questions had pounded her brain over the past few weeks, and still Sally wasn't sure. Not really. She'd always been good at fooling herself, which maybe was why she was so adept at sniffing out fools, a talent that motherhood had only exacerbated.

You can't bullshit a bullshitter, as they say.

A niggling doubt: Did her motivation even matter? Regardless of which way the see-saw rocked, Sally felt she was right to be fearful for Jordan. The world had changed after all, even though the elm tree still stood, seemingly wise and impervious. In truth it was neither.

These were dangerous times.

Trees rot. Sometimes, there were no answers. And bone eaters must bite the dust.

The house peered back at her from beyond the bars, its overgrown lawn seething in the breeze. A murder of crows lined the roof peaks, silhouetted against the clouds like two-dimensional targets in a shooting gallery. Only this gallery had long since closed for business. Cobwebs glazed the windows, deadfall in the driveway. Whatever barkers had thrived here, and not so long ago it felt, had since moved out of town, leaving behind the husk of their carnival. But her toy rifle was loaded still.

One bullet remained.

Shadow against shadow. It darted across the lawn near the side entrance. Sally almost ducked back around the hedge and out of sight, feeling like a spy in one of those late-night espionage movies her husband enjoyed, the kind of films starring crusty middle-aged men in overcoats whose sleuthing was set to dominating scores. Only there was no music here. Just a soundtrack of pulsing blood in her ears, the delightful singsong of a young girl at play.

"Lucette!" she called, waving.

The shadow stilled, and Sally felt it studying her. Another thirty seconds of coaxing saw it emerge into sunlight, taking the shape of a pale pig-tailed girl in a soiled dress holding a dolly. Lucette (who looked thinner than she had at the pharmacy) crossed the lawn to the gate, glanced over her shoulder, back at the cobwebs and murders and, yes, Sally was sure, at the source of all these secrets.

"Hello, sweetheart. It's Sally here."

"I know," the girl said, hands behind her back, swinging her shoulders from side to side. "I've got Miss Natalia here with me." Lucette revealed the limp Raggedy Ann doll.

"I see," Sally said. "How about you let me in, and you, me, and Miss Natalia there can have a tea party. Would you like that?"

"Uh-huh. Sure would."

"Well. Right then, sweetheart. Just wave your magic wand and whisk me through this big old fence of yours. That, or get that delightful mother of yours to come my way and let me in."

Lucette drew Miss Natalia into a hug, squeezing an elongated dog-toy cry from the doll. "I want to, but I'm not allowed to let anyone in. Those are the rules."

Sally knelt down against the pavement, stretching the elasticity of her lycra tights to their limit, and placed the Tupperware container on the cement. Now at eye level, she leaned forward, gripping the bars for balance. "Oh, is that so?"

"Uh-huh."

"You know, sweetheart, it's not polite to lie to people you know," Sally said. "Nothing gets better until the truth is told. Otherwise how else can people like me help you? What's going on? You can tell your Aunty Sally."

"You're not my real aunt."

"Oh, pish-posh. You're like kin to me. You and Miss Natalia both. Your father and I go way back, too. How is he anyway? I hear he's been mighty sick. There's no better medicine than a batch of my world-famous chicken soup."

"You can't help Daddy," the little girl said. "He won't get better."

Sally inhaled, held it, felt herself quiver all over. Exhaled. Her grip on the bars tightened. "Lying's a sin, you know that, right?"

"I have to go back inside now."

"Hold your horses. I bet Miss Natalia knows that lying is bad. I bet she knows that smart girls don't keep secrets from grown-ups. God's always watching."

"I haven't done nothing wrong."

"Then tell me what's happened to your father."

Lucette shuffled from one foot to another. The guilt Sally felt almost drove her to tears, but she clung to the strings of her manipulation, kept the brave smile on her face, though later when she was alone she planned on weakening. A good old-fashioned cry in the shower, away from Conrad. As she so often did.

"Okay, sweetheart," Sally said. "You don't have to tell me anything."

A cloud passed over the sun, paling the air, which in turn, etched definition in the shadows. There, in the yard, where there had only been black, there now were spiders spinning webs and worms churning grit and cold eyes amid the feathers of those crows.

Sally reached through the bars to stroke the leg of the doll.

"I understand why you won't say peep, Lucette. I really do," Sally said, her voice lullaby sweet, despite the wavering. "But would you mind if I asked Miss Natalia a question or two?"

MURPHY'S LAW

EVERY DAY HAS its destiny. The cracking icicle that's almost ready to fall. A branch weighted by too much snow, soon to break. Clouds that try and try to hold in their water, only to fail, and in doing so fulfill their meaning in the world. An architecture of inevitability, that this was *fated* to be. The destiny of this day: Bloodshed. It would begin with a single drop.

A pigeon sailed through the air, uncaring and unthinking. It knew nothing but its desperate need to eat, that desire its only real companion. That, and lice. Wind rustled its feathers as it soared out of the sky towards the hospice, which from above seemed two-dimensional against the snow. It neared the rear courtyard where the tall, two legged creatures sat to eat, this act of survival, despite the cold, uniting them in some strange way.

Closer now. Closer.

It was then that the wind changed, warping the bird's descent. Its wings were sideswiped, its body turning fast. The pigeon didn't feel fear, it had been knocked off course more than once in its day. It understood on a primal level that the sky could be a fickle thing.

The pigeon rolled, trying to flap itself upright again. Only it was too late. It entangled itself in the barbed wire lining the lunch area fence. Metal thorns pierced the bird's fragile hulk, and the more it tried to fight the stronger that hold became. The pigeon screamed until the pain became too much, and then cooed itself into stunned resignation.

Somewhere.

A falling icicle.

A buckling branch.

The coming of the rain.

And there in the hospice courtyard, a single drop of bright red blood pattered against the snow.

***

It was New Year's Day, and whilst all over the country hangovers were nursed and heat-of-the-moment resolutions slowly remembered, Emily found herself back on the merry-go-round, unable to get off. Work. Sober. Riddled with anxiety. She rode it into the break room and found Lucette hunched over the table.

Her daughter was folding paper into origami again, humming to herself in that toneless way kids do. Emily sighed, clenching her jaw, a habit that if she kept up may require medical attention. Her teeth were starting to hurt from the grinding. Despite those shards of adult behavior she often witnessed in Lucette, on that day, her young lady had never looked so childlike.

Like something from a picture book or an illustration from a Dickens' novel, she thought.

It broke Emily's heart to think about what she had to do, and wished she could've left the room right then. The Dickens allusion wasn't lost on Emily, either. Every person went through phases, some of which

hinged upon dependency. Heartbreak made orphans out of all.

No. Emily wouldn't run. To do so would be a cowardly thing. Emily was better than that. But she couldn't muster the courage to say what needed to be said, negating whatever self-respect Emily thought she might have. Not quite yet.

With every fold and crease, Lucette was learning that you could create something from nothing if you worked at it really hard. This in and of itself had the potential to be a beautiful thing. But another lesson lurked within the room, waiting to be taught: with such incredible ease, something—usually *someone*—important in your life could return to that nothingness. *Whoosh*. Gone. Just like that. And this couldn't be helped. No matter how hard you tried. Regardless of the screaming.

Lucette spotted her. "Hey Mom, can I go see Robby now?"

Emily scanned her mind for the right thing to say. She settled on evasion. For now, at least.

Coward. Maybe you're not half the person you think you are.

"I'm pretty sure he's still sleeping," Emily said. Pulse pounding.

"He's been sleeping since we got here."

"I know," she replied, walking over to stroke her daughter's hair. Emily could smell her little girl, that trademark mixture of shampoo, bubblegum, subtle traces of kiddish sweat. These scents made Emily want to hold her, squeeze her. "You have to remember, Robby's a sick boy. He gets worn out."

"Yeah. Okay. Well, I think I've figured out the

crane. I have to show him. Can't we wake him up for a few minutes? I know he wouldn't mind."

"Darlin', he needs his rest. If he wakes before the end of my shift, I'll take you to see him. Otherwise, you'll just have to wait 'til tomorrow."

Lucette stuck her lower lip out in an exaggerated pout and turned back to her paper.

Let her sulk, Emily thought. *As long as she stops asking questions.*

Walking to the fridge, Emily snagged a bottle of water and guzzled it down. Its chill was intense. She could use a *real* drink, something strong and hot and stiff. Gin. But getting sloshed on the job was a sure way to get fired, though it was a common occurrence amongst certain members of the staff. Still, they managed to keep themselves on the payroll.

A whiff of alcohol on the breath, someone tucking away what might have been a phone yet which looked like a flask.

Emily wasn't stupid.

This place could chew you up and make butter of your bones if you didn't find your own way of coping. For some, it was cigarettes, the avarice of so many nurses. For others, it was a sneaky swig here and there. Emily had heard that one of the kitchen hands had been selling his ADHD medication to staff on the floor at an exorbitant price. A hopeful *upper* in a world of downers. Emily understood the appeal, and whilst she wouldn't be treating herself to any of the above, she had little intention of rocking the boat. Hospices, nursing homes, hospitals—they were all the same. You had to cope, and if you didn't, your focus dipped when it was needed most, your perspective on work turned septic. Which was the greater risk, Emily had often debated: the buzz that got you by, even if it violated your duty of care versus abandoning those who needed help because your hair was turning grey from the stress of the job?

Emily wondered about the nature of her vice. She looked down at the girl staring up at her, the one who had seemed so innocent before and smelled of shampoo, bubblegum, and sweat.

You're my carrot on a stick, honey. You get me through. And that's okay. Because at the end of the day, I'm here for you. I promised to keep you safe. Always.

Emily ached for the broken heart the girl would soon suffer. There would be no more visits to see Robby. The boy had taken a turn for the worse the previous evening and wasn't expected to survive the day.

The Crowners had already been sent for.

***

I might be a kid but I'm not stupid.

Of course Lucette knew that Robby was sick and that he needed rest, yet she also knew that sometimes hope and joy were better medicines than whatever it was they put in that plastic bag, the one they fed into the body through a needle. What Robby really needed now was to see that she'd mastered their project, the thing that bound them. Yes, she had mastered the crane, and so would he. Soon enough.

She looked down at the origami. The wings extended out in neat folds; its neck rising high. It sat in the palm of her hand like a delicate flower grown from seed, nurtured in soil that she'd turned herself.

Lucette knew she had a right to be mad. Robby *deserved* to see it.

"I've got to get back to work," Emily said, twisting the cap on the half-empty bottle and stowing it away in the fridge.

"Fine."

"I'll be back to check on you later. Stay here and behave yourself."

Emily was out the door before Lucette could say anything, leaving her to stew in her anger. Why was her mother acting so funny? Come to think of it, *everyone* seemed to have a bee in their bonnet that morning.

Let them be that way.

Old people were weird. This dismissiveness came so easy, sweeping aside her annoyance as though it were little more than the balled up wreckage of her prior origami attempts. She would get the crane to Robby regardless of what her mother said.

***

Mama Metcalf felt jittery today, and she had to play things back to double check if her no-more-than-one-coffee-a-day rule had been broken. She was certain she hadn't over-indulged. Yet her heart still fluttered in her chest, a bird beating against the bars of its cage. Every noise startled. Only ten minutes ago Mykel had dropped a breakfast tray in the hallway leading towards the common dining area and she'd near leapt right out of her skin. But the source of her edginess was lost on her.

Except that wasn't true. She just didn't want to acknowledge it.

Several factors contributed to her current mood,

not least of which was the oppressive atmosphere in the hospice because of little Robby's condition. It was as though the snow clouds building outside had wormed their way into the building, churning on the ceiling, threatening to pour down on them. On top of that, the mob that always congregated outside had been aggressive that morning. More so than usual. Mama Metcalf had no idea how people mustered the energy, day after day, to maintain the futility of their anger when it always added up to nothing. The protesters could yell and chant and wave their hateful signs until the cows came home, and still all that hot air would account for diddly-squat. The sick still needed to be cared for. The machine still had to turn. And she was proud to be one of the many cogs, even on bad days.

The door swung open and Emily stepped out as Mama Metcalf approached the FSU. Beyond the young woman the corridor stretched off to that awful room at the end, the penultimate stop for all of their guests. That was where the crown was kept.

"How's he doing?" Mama Metcalf asked.

Even with the mask covering the lower half of her face, Emily's expression answered the question before she spoke. "He's still conscious, which in this case may not be a blessing. He's in a semi-delirious state. I'm not sure he's fully aware of where he is or what's happening. At one point he started calling for his mother. Fuck, that hurt to hear."

"Has anyone contacted his parents? Told them it's time?"

"Woods has left several messages, but surprise-surprise, they haven't responded. They haven't been to see him once, so I don't know why we should expect them to show up now."

"Well, he shouldn't have to go through this experience alone. I'm gonna talk to Woods about me being there when the Crowners take him."

Emily shook her head. "I already asked. She said since he was a minor, we'd have to have parental consent to do that."

"This ain't right. A young'un shouldn't have to die alone, nothing but strangers in the room. Since he's been here, we're the closest thing to family he's got."

"I know, but Woods says the law is clear. We could get shut down if we don't follow it to the letter. Even if she wanted to look the other way, no way the Crowners would go for it. They're Ministry officials, after all."

"Ministry folks are still just people when you get down to it."

"I'm not so sure about that. As far as I'm concerned, they can stick their policies and procedures up their wazoos. Sideways, if you like."

The women lapsed into silence, leaning against the wall.

Mama Metcalf thought of her Erik. There was nothing like death to make you want to cling to what little you had left. She had to do something to bridge the gap that existed between them. The days she had left to spend with her son were likely few and she refused to let them slip by without putting up a fight—she was a Metcalf after all and wasn't above wrangling that which needed to be wrangled. And if that meant she had to force Erik to spend time with her then so be it. He'd be thankful for it someday. Her efforts wouldn't be like those of the protesters outside; it wouldn't just be more hot air in an otherwise cold world. Something would come of it. Of that she was sure.

Got to make the most of it. Always. Just like that darlin' Lucette did with Robby.

Good Lord, that girl has got a world of hurt coming her way.

"What you two doing loitering about?" Mama Metcalf tensed at the sound of Mykel's sing-song voice as he approached them from the adjoining corridor.

"Must you be so chipper?" Emily said.

"I'm sorry, have they passed some law against being happy in the workplace?"

"This ain't a happy kinda day," Mama Metcalf said. "It's a 'maybe I ought-a take a smoke break again' kind of day, 'cause God only knows I need something to get me through it."

"Why? Because of the kid? It's not like we didn't know this was how it would end."

"Jesus," Emily said, and Mama Metcalf noticed her hands were balled into fists at her side. "Do you think you could muster just the tiniest drop of sensitivity? I mean, don't strain yourself or anything, but come on. Try."

"Hey, I'm not being insensitive, just *realistic*. This is a hospice; it isn't a place people come to get better. Every person who walks through that door leaves in a body bag. That's the reality, and if you can't deal with that then you might be in the wrong line of work."

Emily pushed past him and stalked down the hall. Not wanting to be alone with Mykel, Mama Metcalf punched in the code to open the door to the FSU and hurried through. As the door swung shut behind her, she heard him say, "Fine, be that way! Break down into a snail trail of tears and estrogen every time the inevitable happens."

Mama Metcalf paused, putting a hand to the wall to steady herself. With eyes closed, she took a few shaky breaths through the mask, trying to calm herself. The thing that upset her most was that, despite the tactless delivery, Mykel was correct, hence the tell-tale 'F' in FSU. Emotional callouses from the bedpans, pity, and death kept him immune. That way sorrow passed him over, all thunder but no lightning.

God, she hoped she never reached that point. Let her heart never grow that hard.

With a final deep breath, Mama Metcalf started toward Robby's room, thinking that during her break she would call Erik and tell him she was coming over for a visit this evening whether he wanted her to or not.

***

Robby's body let him in on a secret: You're dying. It wasn't as painful as he'd expected it to be in all honesty, maybe even less severe than the worst of his night fevers. He could sense himself winding down, every ambition evaporated from his will by the heat that had brought him to this moment.

Dinosaur bones. Exploration. Girls.

All of it had been steamed away. He was no longer sad. Just grateful.

If the uglies were here they hid in his joints, in those wet spaces between his bones and skin, dancing with accomplishment. He wanted to scratch at them but couldn't move. His teeth hurt worst of all. Sweat dripped into his eyes. Lifting a finger to wipe the beads away wasn't going to happen though. Even blinking was an effort; and when he did, each flutter worsened his vision. There were people in the room, blurry silhouettes going here and there, haloed by kaleidoscopes of refracted light.

A sound in his throat. Rattlesnake breaths.

Robby thought he could feel hands on him, grasping and clawing and groping. He wondered if he was still in the hospice room.

No. He wasn't.

He was in the woods behind the fairgrounds on the night of the Halloween festival. The homeless man had him in his grip again, leaving Robby to wonder if he'd ever escaped in the first place. Being abandoned by his family, the embarrassment of having people he didn't know bathe him, Lucette and her origami fixation—maybe it all had been a dream. A fantasy. He was still at the bottom of the ravine, just another kid versus a vicious, adult world.

Voices. Faraway. It was the people at the festival, laughing and chattering. So close.

Robby blinked harder than before and the fog cleared. He wasn't in the woods, but back in his over-lit hospice room, of course. The machines around him were beeping, there were needles jabbed into his arms. Tubes crisscrossed his chest, carrying liquid left and right. An old woman stared down at him.

Unable to speak, Robby willed her name.

Mama Metcalf.

And even though he could see her face, the creases of her skin like freeways in a roadmap of places he would never travel, those distant voices continued to chime. They were nearer now. Louder. They held a jeering, hateful quality.

It was then that Robby understood. The sound wasn't the memory of those at the Halloween fair. It was the voice of the mob congregated outside.

Uglies of a different breed.

***

Words like an oil slick over water, catching the sunlight in shapeless swirls. None of the paperwork made sense, leaving Woods rubbing her head. She had another one of her headaches, a Grade A doozie, the kind that sent her rummaging around for an Aspirin to chew on. She liked everything to be in order when the Crowners were coming, but concentrating on the reams of paper splayed across the table was impossible to do with the chants of the mob echoing down the corridor.

They were always out there, though the numbers waxed and waned. Today, however, the crowd was bigger than she'd ever seen it before. Stupid people with their stupid New Year's resolutions, fools following fools. Woods hoped the sky opened up and shat snow over all of them, cooling their hatred, scattering doses of frostbite as it went.

Were she completely honest with herself, her annoyance had less to do with the protestors and more to do with today's duty. Losing a guest was always difficult, but it was particularly rough when that guest had no loved ones to help ease him or her through the transition.

Ha. The 'transition'. Like 'guest', it's just another pathetic mask.

Woods' job was to make sure that mask didn't slip, not on her face or any of those working under her wing. This was easier said than done when one of her headaches had crawled inside her skull and made itself at home.

Emily passed in the hall and Woods called her name.

"What's up?" Emily asked, taking a seat after closing the door.

Woods took a deep breath, recognized she was about to jump off the point of no return, and made the leap anyway. Some things just had to be done. "I've changed my mind."

"About what?"

"You asked if you could go with Robby when the Crowners take him."

"You said that was impossible without parental consent."

"You got it." Woods handed Emily a consent form with Mrs. Hopkins' name scrawled at the bottom.

"You mean she showed up?"

Woods shook her head.

"Then how? Wait, do you mean that you—"

"He shouldn't be alone, and I know he bonded with you and your daughter. If his real family can't be bothered to be here, someone has to step up."

"Mrs. Woods, I don't know what to say."

"Then don't say anything. Just be there, hold his hand. Let him know he's loved."

Emily nodded, staring down at the form. "I haven't told Lucette yet. I thought it might be better to wait until after."

"When the time comes, I'll bring her in my office, try to keep her occupied."

"I appreciate that."

Emily stood and started from the room but Woods

said, "I need the form to give to the Crowners when they arrive."

"Oh, of course." Emily placed the paper back on the desk, left.

Once Woods was alone again, she sat with her hands on the top of her desk and watched them shake, finally placing them in her lap as if to hide the evidence of her unsettled nerves. She'd always been willing to bend the rules from time to time in the pursuit of dignity, but forging Mrs. Hopkins' name went beyond minor infractions of policy and protocol.

She'd leapt past the point of no return, splashing into dangerous waters. Shark-like felonies lurked amongst the waves. And what sharp teeth they had.

***

Betty Hopkins wasn't built for a lot of things.

Despite her three-and-a-half decades living in Chicago, the construction of her tolerance didn't extend to winter. She hated the cold—downright *deplored* it—and in turn, hated herself for not being able to adapt to each seasonal lashing. Yet here she was.

Betty also didn't think she was built to handle large crowds. All of those gnarled faces knitted together. It made her stomach knot, drew black dots over her vision that swam like mosquito larvae across the surface of a pond—just like the one she and her sisters had paddled in as kids. Not that Betty saw much of her family anymore, let alone the pond at the rear of her parents' property. Everywhere she turned there was nothing but the twisted wreckage of burnt bridges, with her husband, more often than not, the arsonist. And yet here she was. Out in the cold, escaping the crowd.

Finally, and with a melancholy that surpassed everything else, Betty Hopkins didn't think she was built for motherhood. It had come so naturally to her sisters, women whose smiles of affection appeared so genuine, smiles replicated in their children as they ran and played at their grandparents' place, splish-splashing in that same pond. And yet here she was. Out in the cold, escaping the crowd, still a mother despite not having seen her child in so long.

All because of my husband.

This was what she told herself. That Tim was to blame. Though it was hard to tell if that was entirely the truth.

One thing that Betty *was* good at was the ancient art of second-guessing herself. She was doing so that very moment, there on the sidewalk, two blocks from the hospice.

Tim is the one who made all this ugliness a reality. At least I think it was him. Please don't tell me I played a part. Please.

Quivering hands struck a match. Lit the cigarette. A flicker of heat against her palms, and then it was gone. The dead matchstick tumbled to the slush between her boots as smoke filled her lungs. Betty told herself that she'd quit when she was dead.

And maybe not even then.

Second thoughts.

Robby was her son, and it wasn't right that she not be by his side when—God, she couldn't even *think* the word. This couldn't be her life, could it?

He had been such a tiny, meek child.

And it wasn't Robby's fault. He hadn't asked for this. But that wasn't how Tim saw it. He blamed the boy for being where he shouldn't have been; saw what happened almost as God's punishment. She didn't know if her husband truly believed this, or if it was just a cracked way of trying to cope with tragedy. Betty wondered if things would have turned out differently if Robby had contracted the infection any other way. Bitten on the street as opposed to—

(say it)

—raped by a stranger.

(dear God, why would you do this to us, to him)

Robby had confessed what really happened to her alone, and then she'd taken the revelation to her husband. Betty hadn't had much respect left for Tim and his reaction to the truth destroyed what little remained. Congratulations—he was now the father of a tainted thing. Were Robby to have been simply violated and not infected, Betty believed Tim *still* would have excommunicated the boy. So deeply rooted was his fear of anything remotely gay.

Men can be such prideful pigs.

So stand up to him then!

This was easier said than done. This wasn't the time of *Father Knows Best* or *Leave it to Beaver*, where the dutiful wife had to defer to her husband's will, but she knew that if she truly questioned Tim on this it would lead to a blowout that would cause their marriage to crumble. As appalled as she was by her husband, she couldn't run the risk of losing him and Robby all at the same time. What would be left then?

But Tim didn't have to know about her trip to the hospice. When they'd received the first message from Mrs. Woods, he'd run off, no doubt to Duvall's Bar where he spent more of his time lately. She didn't expect to see him again until tonight. Would he come in pretending nothing had happened, that it was just another day, or would they talk about it? And if this unlikely second option happened, what would Betty say? Would she admit to coming to the hospice to help her son when he needed it most, to be with the defective goods they had thrown away?

Admit to coming here to prove she was a better person than she believed she really was?

As Betty came within sight of the hospice, finishing her cigarette, head tucked beneath the collar of her overcoat, her footsteps faltered. There were protesters gathered around out front, waving their signs and polluting the air with their hateful words. To think, she and Tim had once been a part of that crowd.

Though neither had been back since Robby fell sick.

Betty stopped a block away, pushing herself against the wall of an adjoining liquor store. She was bound to know some of the people. Were she recognized then word would filter back to Tim. Of this she had no doubt. When she'd left the house, Betty had considered wearing sunglasses and a headscarf to disguise her appearance, but dismissed this option on account of it being totally fucking insane. Now she thought otherwise.

"Betty?"

Hearing her name caused her to jerk and clutch her purse. She looked back toward the protestors to see who had spotted her and gasped when she saw Tim detach himself from the crowd and walk toward her. He wore his I'VE GOT MOXIE cap, the one he'd re-gifted to his son only to reclaim it back when the boy proved himself obsolete. Waste not, want not.

"Betty, what are you doing here?"

She couldn't speak, didn't know what to say. Tim carried a sign reading, BONE EATERS R NOT PEOPLE & DON'T DESERVE RIGHTS!

He stood in front of her now, that sign leaned casually over one shoulder as though it was something as innocuous as an umbrella.

"Answer me," he said. "What are you doing here?"

Tell him!

(Tell him what?)

Tell him that we've both been ridiculous. That it's not too late to change. Robby needs us.

Tim grabbed her arm and twisted it, causing her to cry out. "Half our church is over there watching. Tell me right this goddamn minute what you're doing here?"

"I. Well, you see. I came to join you."

"How did you even know I was here?"

Tim didn't move or speak, leaving Betty shaking under his grip. She thought about wringing herself free and running down the semi-frozen sidewalk, running all the way to one of her sister's houses on the other side of the city if need be. Only she didn't. Betty stood her ground, matching her husband's glare.

"I—" Her unfinished whisper steam-stained the air.

Came here for our son. To be with him. To be braver than you ever could be or ever were, Tim. You're a fucking disgusting piece of shit for making me this way.

Say it.

SAY IT.

"—I figured this was where you'd be, and I thought we should be together," Betty said, second-guessing herself again. She yanked her arm free and held her head high. It was almost enough to make her laugh. Who needed a silly disguise when one was already so adept at wearing the mask of complacency?

Tim melted, enveloped his wife in an awkward hug. "I knew you'd come round. Robby died Halloween night, and *them* keeping his corpse here makes it impossible to grieve and move on. The Ministry has gone soft. They used to take care of it the humane way. You see that now, right?"

Betty nodded, forcing a smile.

"Come on, everyone will be so glad to see you."

She allowed her husband to take her hand and pull her back to the group. Several faces she recognized from church, another from behind the pulpit. They greeted her with handshakes and hugs, their affection a stark contrast to the epitaphs on their signs.

"Betty, it's wonderful to have you back in the fold," said an old woman with ratty gray hair and a worn dress. It was black, as it always was. Betty couldn't remember her name—was it Mabry? *Yes, I think so.* Betty knew the woman's own son had been in the hospice and had died shortly after Robby was admitted.

A chill ran through Betty's body. She wondered if this was what hatred turned you into. A wraith-like creature warmed only by clichés, a woman whose face was frozen in that moment of terrible darkness that preceded a relief that would never come. "The dead roam those halls," Mabry said, a B-movie line that Betty had heard from those lizardy lips more than once. It unnerved her then as it always had.

Because on some level it was true.

"It's good to be back," Betty said, each word broken glass in her mouth.

"I know what you're going through," the old woman said. Her eyes held no shimmer or life, they were like dead stars overlooking a cracked, dry desert. "They put my Edward in there, pumped him full of chemicals and kept his body moving long after he was dead. It's sacrilegious is what it is, not to mention dangerous. Keeping these demons around puts us all at risk."

"Demons?"

"Our children die, and then demons crawl up in their bodies and wear them like a suit."

Betty looked around at those nearby, including her husband. Nobody was reacting as though Mabry were some crazy cat lady in a comic skit. No. They were nodding. Even Tim. She was surrounded by lunatics.

And now I'm in their number.

The old woman leaned forward and wrapped her claws around Betty's wrist. She appeared so wiry and small, only the strength in that grip was as frightening as anything Betty had ever experienced. Fear made people weak, this she knew better than most, but in turn, nothing fueled the human body better than hatred. And the more unfounded that hatred was, the better the mileage.

Mabry crooned in Betty's ear. Her breath like dead mice in a crawlspace. "The abomination ends."

Before Betty could ask the woman what she meant by that, the crowd swallowed them alive. In the heat of their guts, Tim planted a kiss on Betty's lips, more passionate than any since before Robby was born.

"We'll get you a sign," he said.

***

The group gathered in front of the hospice wasn't even worthy of a sigh, but Geraldine gave one anyway. Every time the five of them had come to perform their duty, the crowd always seemed a little bigger than it had the time before, more threatening. But she'd never seen it swelled to such numbers. They teemed like a river about to break its bank, and when it did, Geraldine had no doubt that sinners and saviors would be drowned alike.

"Great, just what we need today," grumbled one of the Ministry workers at her side. Geraldine couldn't remember his name, but she understood his trepidation and gave his arm a polite squeeze. She wasn't here to make friends, so her cohort shouldn't expect additional pandering, but a healthy amount of condescension would make this journey easier.

The Crowners' responsibility was destined to be difficult, though Geraldine had to admit the burden felt heavier today. They were here to 'counsel' a child.

As they approached the protestors, the group turned their ire from the imposing cement walls of the hospice and onto them. Insults and curses stoned them from every direction, all screamed in the name of the same God Geraldine clung to. But beneath her layman's camouflage—the tattered woolen scarf, her scuffed shoes—there was more than governmental policy steeling her resolve. There was resentment, crusted over like a protective scrim. The source of her bitterness was how two people could read the same text and interpret the words so differently.

And yet they don't realize the truth of it all. Go on, scream and shout. Hate until you're blue in the face.

It all ends the same way. One way or another, we all kneel before the crown.

The five reached the steps. Geraldine felt something wet slap her cheek and realized someone had just spat on her. She glanced over to see an old woman in black laughing and pointing at her. A sudden wind whipped through the crowd and sent the spitter's gown fluttering on her frame, her gray hair like Medusa's snakes, revealing the boyish sneakers on her feet. Geraldine refused to give the bitch the satisfaction of watching her wipe the phlegm away. She wore it like a tattoo right up to the front door, at which the head administrator, Woods, was standing.

The Crowners hurried inside.

***

The passage of time was no longer marked by anniversaries or birthdays for Wanda Mabry, rather in pockmarks from surgeries dug from the flesh beneath her dress. Her body was riddled with Melanomas, and come March, she was scheduled to go under the knife again. The snarled clusters of cancers clung to her system, growing fat, telemarked above by a blemish or mole. But with time they spored, a bullet in the blood seeking out fresh places to corrupt.

The allusion was not lost on her.

She broke away from the group, and when she was sure no one was watching, ducked down the narrow alley that ran around to the back of the building. Her white sport sneakers, a new pair that she'd picked up two weeks ago with the remainder of her pension, splashed through sludge. She cradled her handbag as she went.

Steam seeped into the air from a nearby sewer grate.

The side of the hospice barrier was covered in a lattice of graffiti, phalluses, smiley faces, names, and words that made no sense to Wanda on any level. She stopped to catch her breath, one of her strong hands against the wall. Through her fingers she read a small vignette:

Time to go, no time to grieve. If it doesn't end now we'll never leave.

She shuddered. It was as though the poet had come to this very place, carved the rant upon the wall, and known that someday in the future she would come along in her brand new sneakers, and feed off the motivation. It nourished her when she needed it most. She had to do what she'd needed to do for so long. But doubt, like her cancers, spread fast.

She thought of her dead husband. The living sons who no longer spoke to her. Of the poet. Yes. It was time.

Wanda approached the trashcans piled against the wall. She'd moved them to that position in late November, though her plan had been mapped out months before. For a long time Wanda wondered if she would ever go through with it, but as she sat in her tiny apartment the night before to watch the ball drop on her television, sipping Vodka from a teacup and chewing pickled cabbage, she realized some resolutions *had* to come to fruition.

The world was a cancer victim. Nobody lived forever. It was important to do what we were put on this earth to do, and then let ourselves be taken into the arms of the Almighty. This she believed more than anything else.

Wanda turned to face the wall and saw the barbs at the top. A black cat was wrestling with the remains of a half frozen pigeon entangled in the wire. Small pointy teeth speared the carcass, yanking it sideways. A single feather rode the wind and vanished up the alley. The cat lost its footing and landed on its feet in the virgin snow next to Wanda's sneaker-prints, followed half a beat later by the bird itself. Those dead eyes stared up at her as the cat spirited it away.

***

Mama Metcalf sat by herself in the courtyard outside of the break room, puffing on a hand-rolled cigarette. The echoes of traffic combined with protestor chants could be heard from here, a constant bee-drone that almost made her sleepy. Her cell was on the bench beside her, its silence plus the nicotine buzz keeping her awake. It was an old brick of a phone that Erik had bought for her so they could keep in contact, which she'd attempted to do not ten minutes ago only to be told that he was too busy to talk and would call her back later. This was a promise that he'd made many times before, and almost never followed through on. The screen glared up at her, a green window into a room she was only *sometimes* invited.

"Not this time," she murmured.

Come hell or high water she would be knocking on his door after work. Sure, there was a possibility that he might see her visit for what it was—an ambush—but Mama Metcalf was confident in her ability to frame it as the kind of surprise 'you didn't know you needed 'til it arrived'. Desperation had made a truth-tweaker out of her more than once. Today would be no different.

Mama Metcalf stubbed her cigarette on the bottom

of her shoe, the sensation of squishing it into an ashy mess weirdly satisfying as always, and put the butt in the plastic sandwich baggie she'd brought with her. She laced her fingers together and tilted her head skyward. The clouds parted to let through some sunlight. It was still as cold as a witch's tit out here though. Summer had never felt so far away. Once it was warmer she might stay with Erik for a while, or propose a short vacation together. Somewhere outdoorsy. She'd always wanted to see the great redwood forest on the outskirts of San Francisco, passing through their shade and out into the open where the Golden Gate Bridge, she'd been told, was on proud display. Mama Metcalf made a note of talking to her son about it that evening.

The cell phone display reflected the sunlight. Though not for long. Those heavy clouds rolled across the sky again. Over, done with, gone. For now, at least.

She was readying herself to get back into the hospice where she would fill up her medication trolley and complete her rounds when she heard a scraping from the wall enclosing the smoking area. This was followed by banging, crunching tin. Grunting. A frown creased her already wrinkled forehead.

Oh, for crying in a bucket. What now?

Mama Metcalf stepped away from the picnic table and drew her coat close to her neck. She strode over to the wall and glanced up as a black jacket came sailing over its upper edge, catching on the barbed wire fringe.

Turn away now, said a voice in the back of her head. That terrible unease that had been with her since the moment she stepped inside the hospice roiled again, churning her senses. But she didn't turn away, and instead stood there, watching with her mouth open as a pair of hands clawed at the jacket from the other side.

"Now-now-now!" Mama Metcalf said, waving at the intruder and shuffling on the spot. "Don't you go and do that." She felt useless and silly the way she was carrying on, but there was nothing else to do.

Churning. *Churning.*

A woman in a black dress began to pull herself up over the wall using the jacket to protect herself from the barbs. An old face peered down at her; the expression warped by what surely must be an arthritis-aggravating contortion. Just looking at her made Mama Metcalf ache. The breeze whipped the old woman's hair until it covered half of her face like a veil. She couldn't believe what she was seeing. The woman climbing over the fence very well may be as old as Mama Metcalf, but unlike her, this stranger had a coarse strength to her.

"Hey, you get down from there. You're going to hurt yourself."

As if her words caused it to happen, the woman slipped and her left forearm slit open on the barbed wire. Blood rushed in a torrent, freckling the snow. Mama Metcalf gave a yell, knowing too well how easily the papery skin of those who were long-in-the-tooth ripped, and watched as the stranger toppled forward, cutting up her legs in the process. Her dress—so black and tight fitting, like something people with little imagination wore to funerals—snagged on the spikes, exposing her slip as she fell to the ground. Mama Metcalf figured the fall itself might have done some serious damage if last night's snow hadn't left a bed of white for her to land in. Having worked as a volunteer at the hospice for as long as she had, and being as old as she was, Mama Metcalf knew how easy it was to break a hip. Hell, old folks did it sitting down on the commode too damn hard. Let alone *this*.

"You foolish thing! Are you okay?" Mama Metcalf said, rushing to the woman's side. An almost electric shock of recognition hit her then: this was one of the protestors from outside, the crone who sometimes spat at them. The one who seemed to hate them for their compassion worst of all. Mama Metcalf knew she should run back inside and call for help, but it was in her DNA to not leave. Not yet. When someone was in need, she had to reach out. Her emergency response training unraveled before her.

Check for immediate danger—downed power lines, spilled water, that kind of thing. Nope, skip this part. It wasn't relevant. The old bat had done this to herself. Next: assess the victim. Check for a pulse, identify the issues, and *then* seek help.

The old woman snapped herself around at a speed that made Mama Metcalf's heart skip a beat. She was almost sure she'd heard the crunch and grind of bones popping as the sinewy frame uncoiled in front of her, kicking snow with those funny looking sneakers, with those clawed hands reaching for her purse. An image came to Mama Metcalf's mind just then. A snake, readying itself to strike. Fangs dripping venom.

It happened so fast.

Those pale eyes rose to meet Mama Metcalf's. Lips parted to let out the stink of her words. "The devil comes in the guise of an angel," the woman said, raising her right hand.

Mama Metcalf recognized the object in that hand as a gun an instant before the report. The noise came as a shock, a clap of thunder through an open, sunny field. It was tremendously *immediate*. She felt like someone had smacked her across the back of her neck. Mama Metcalf touched her throat and felt something peculiar there, a flower with fleshy petals peeling back. Red rain showered down from the sky to douse the old woman with the gun, coloring the snow about them. A moment later Mama Metcalf realized the rain was coming from that flower. Sizzling arcs draped the picnic area like the Christmas tinsel still adorning the walls of her house.

She fell backwards, head rapping the ground. It was the sensation of being winded that caused her to panic. There was no pain otherwise. Only that sky up above, the clouds drawing back to let through a little warmth again. Just enough to tickle her nose and make her squint. She thought of the light through redwood trees growing brighter as she neared the clearing where the Golden Gate bridge could be seen.

An odd numbness began to spread throughout her body, sweeping away the image of those tall trees. Soon there was only the sky again. The clouds parted further, and when Mama Metcalf tried to raise a hand to shield her eyes she found that she couldn't muster the strength. That numbness had her in its hold now, and she feared it would never let go.

She didn't need to worry about the glare for long. The light was eclipsed by a figure. The sun crafted a halo from its hair. Arms like those of a great black bird, or maybe those of a man. A man who wanted to hug her. His invitation was strong.

"Erik," Mama Metcalf said, gurgling on coppery blood.

You came to see me. I'm so—

***

The old woman shot her in the face.

***

Mykel heard the *pop* over the ding-dong of overlapping emergency buzzer alerts from where he was standing, slipping off a pair of latex gloves, in the corridor leading to the break room. Even though he knew it made no sense at all, he could have sworn someone had just set off a firecracker in the courtyard. He hurried down the hall, passed through the empty kitchenette and glanced out the glass door on the left. Mykel wasn't sure what he expected to find, perhaps the sizzling remains of someone's New Year's poppers propped up in the snow. Only no. That was not what was out there.

It took a moment for him to comprehend what he was seeing. When it clicked, he felt a tiny trickle of urine slip into his underwear.

Mama Metcalf was lying on the ground, her face like a punched in Halloween pumpkin, surrounded by wings of crimson snow. Another old woman—this one in a torn black dress—stood over her. Mykel's paralysis broke when he saw the gun in her hand.

He yelled back into the building for help as he pushed through the door and sprinted across the courtyard. The woman in black unloaded another shot into Mama Metcalf's head. More starbursts of blood. Mykel tackled the old woman to the ground, wondering the whole time, *What the fuck am I doing here? I'm no hero.*

That was your brother. Remember?

The world became a shaken up snow globe as they rolled, fighting against one another. Red slop splashed into Mykel's mouth and he hardly noticed. Adrenaline eclipsed all else. The woman—who looked like someone out of a Grimm's fairy tale illustration, an old witch ready to lure children into her oven—was so damn strong. This caught him off guard. As did her scream, which was angry, primal. She tried to raise the gun again. He snatched her wrist, his whole hand wrapping around her bones, and banged it against the leg of the picnic table. The woman cried out. Dropped the weapon. Mykel kicked it away and laid the full weight of his body on her frame, making sure she couldn't scramble free.

"You cunt!" the woman screeched. "Cunt!"

"Stop. Christ, what've you done? Fuck. Fuck." And then to the sky, spittle flying: "HELP! Someone help me!"

Behind him he heard shouting voices. Footsteps. He prayed they were running towards him, not away.

***

Lucette backed against the wall outside Corridor 3. An alarm started to bleat from speakers she couldn't see, making her clutch the near-perfect crane to her chest as though shielding it from the noise. Down the hallway she saw her mother and Woods skirt from one of the building's arteries and into another, their faces matching portraits of confusion. Other nurses bustled about.

The alarm was loud, frightening. It sounded like a wounded animal screeching over and over again, a vulture from one of those environmental documentaries her teachers made them watch at school on rainy sports days. The overhead bulbs dimmed and secondary lights, all red, flicked on. Lucette told herself to be a big girl, be brave. She figured there must be an emergency somewhere, and as sad as that may be for those involved, it was the perfect distraction for her.

She scuttled closer to the door leading to the FSU, stopping to glance over her shoulder and make sure she hadn't been seen. *So far so good.* Lucette flicked bangs out of her eyes and reached up to punch in the code she remembered her mother using. Hopefully it hadn't been changed since that day.

67845 followed by the # key.

Was Lucette aware that she was doing something naughty? Yes, of course she was. But like the day she'd pretended to be a bone-eater at school (or a zombie, or a smiler—whatever she was or was not supposed to call them) she sensed that going to visit Robby was the *right* thing to do. Even if it meant doing a wrong. She clenched her jaw and braved the keypad, resenting the adults of the world who spoke as though their rules were simple when in fact they were anything but. More than anything, Lucette had come to believe that there were special times when people needed to know that they were being mean to someone, like the kids in her class who had made fun of her. And in turn, there were times when people needed to know they were appreciated. People like Robby.

Though it had been she who made the crane in the end, it was he who had earned it.

Buttons clicked and clacked under the tip of her index finger and she was relieved when she heard the lock unlatch from the jam. Not knowing if she was going to encounter anyone on the other side, Lucette decided her best course of action was to act like she belonged here, to stare straight ahead and walk with a steady, confident gait.

The ruse wasn't necessary as it turned out. The hall on the other side of the door was deserted, bathed in that scarlet glow. She crept forward, drawn to soft moaning, soft weeping, which came from the room on her right and somehow managed to slit through the screech of the alarm. Lucette edged closer to the door, hands gripping the architrave. Peered in.

Her mouth went dry. Eyes widened.

She'd heard their names bandied about in FSU by nurses coming and going between the rooms. From memory, they were Speedy and Tammy—though she may have heard wrong. The man was sitting on the edge of the bed next to an empty wheelchair and the woman was on her knees between his legs. The back of her hospital gown was open, the rise and fall of her spine casting its own shadow in the red light; it almost hurt to look at. Their bodies were woven with IV tubes. Lucette clung to the architrave tighter; not quite understanding what she was seeing but drawing the dots together. The woman had Speedy's pee-pee (*no, say it right, it's a penis*) in her mouth and was bouncing her lips up and down on it, making the man grunt. Or was he crying?

Lucette thought to herself, *They're doing the thing that makes babies. Though it's not what I'd heard. They're doing it differently. Or maybe the girls at school were wrong.*

The sight intrigued as it terrified. She sensed that

something was clicking in her mind, a final turning cog falling into place. This was what it was to be a man and a woman. And even though it sent her stomach into rollercoaster lurches, Lucette knew she had no choice but accept it. Everyone was born. Everyone grew up. Everyone did what everyone does. And then you die, just as her father had died. Just as Robby would, too.

And one day, so will I.

Beginning and end linked through bodies in strange and sickening ways. It made no sense, yet made complete sense at the same time.

The two stick figures in the room stilled, drew up their heads and turned to face her, each moving at the same slow pace. They looked like automated Christmas decorations in a storefront window, robots without emotion contorted into painful positions for the benefit of others. Their eyes were almost dead, and seemed not to care that they had been observed. Tammy, tears on her cheeks despite the rictus smile, turned back to Speedy's penis and swallowed it whole.

Screech. Screech. Screech.

Lucette backed away, afraid. She ran to Robby's room and bolted through the door, holding up the crane. In her head it became a talisman. Something to keep her strong, whilst still keeping her young.

She skidded to a halt. Robby was drenched in sweat, as were his sheets. He thrashed on the mattress. His breathing was shallow, clambering for air.

"Oh, Robby," she said. "No."

This was what her mother had been hiding from her. On some level Lucette had known all along and had been pretending it wasn't so. This was the F and S alluded to in the FSU sign mounted into the wall beside the keypad she'd hacked. The final stage.

Lucette didn't know if she loved or hated her mother in that moment, as the lights burned red and the vultures called. There were lies wherever she looked, as unavoidable as shadows. There was no Santa Claus, no Tooth Fairy—only wrongs and rights intersecting in ways nobody had stopped to warn her about.

She looked down at her imperfect crane and realized how silly it was. It wasn't going to change anything. It wasn't going to save anyone.

Robby's thrashing ceased the moment she let the crane drop. His breathing drew into a long rattle. She crushed the origami beneath her sneaker as she neared the bed, watching her friend die in front of her.

Lucette knew she should call for someone—the alert buzzer was right there—and yet all she could think about was the day she'd created summer for him, with Robby musing about all the things he'd never get to do. It hadn't seemed real to her then. The fantasy had been as much for her benefit as it was for him.

Like their dream, Robby was almost gone.

His eyes no longer blinked, the last of his lashes cast across his cheeks. He lay there, bald and broken, white as the ghost he soon would become, smiling up at her. She thought, just maybe, that there was a flicker of recognition in his face, that yes—he knew he wasn't alone. Although this may have been wishful thinking.

Lucette wanted to do the right thing. There was still enough time to give him a gift while he was still here. Something a lot better than a sheet of folded paper.

She leaned forward to give him a kiss.

There were no fairytale illusions that this would restore him to health as always happened in cartoons. There was only the act itself: a much-delayed sliver of reality at the end of their summer. It would not fade as her drawn-on leaves had in the frosted window. This gift would linger, and hopefully Robby would take it with him wherever he ended up.

***

Eternity in a cup of cocoa. The answers to all questions in a single fortune cookie. No faces, yet every face at the same time. It all came rushing at him, the *enormity* of it all. And for the first time in so long he knew relief. It severed him from his body, whooshing away all of the pain that had come to define him.

The uglies were there with him, only they didn't claw or scratch. They stood around him in a vigil, no longer scary, breathing in unison. The longer they stood there the more their expressions blurred. Soon they were just eyes and mouths, though not even this lasted. He watched them fade into the red, and despite everything that had happened, Robby missed their assaults.

Now there was only the face lowering itself over him. It was as big as the moon.

He smelled her. She was delicious.

Like a baby turning its tongue to its mother's tit for the first time. Like someone shielding themselves from flame. His hunger was not learned, it was simply known.

***

Lucette kissed the taut pull of her friend's lips.

And he bit hers off in return.

INTERLUDE SIX

To complete, inside reverse fold one side to fashion the head, and then fold down the wings. Only then, as you do this, will the origami crane take shape. You are finished.

EMILY WAS IN the bed she no longer shared with her husband, yet which still smelled like him, when the noise came. Twisting metal, shrieking tires, engines that roared like rabid things hell-bent on biting and tearing until there was nothing left to bite and tear. Whoever they were, they had knocked down the gate. All that noise was lightning-fierce, seeming to shake the earth their house was built on, snapping her from sleep. It extinguished all other sound. She bolted upright, unable to hold in or hear her cry, and watched the window overlooking the driveway burn bright, the venetian blinds sending swirling bars of yellow light across the walls. Emily shielded her face, splayed fingers doing little to obscure that false-dawn glare.

Doors slammed. The thump of heavy boots pounding the lawn.

She looked at the closed bedroom door, imagined the hallway just outside leading to the spare room where her husband would by lying, hopefully doped up enough that the edge of his agony was blunted. She feared for him, now more than ever, as she felt the thunder-thrum of strangers breaking into the house.

Emily screamed Jordan's name, throwing back the blankets, leaping off the mattress and bumping the bedside table in the process. A half-empty glass of water overturned and shattered against the floorboards, shards pin-wheeling here and there. The world spun on a dizzy axis for a few beats and she steadied herself against the door, face flush with the wood. Her head settled. Emily gripped the handle, knowing that the moment she turned it her world would change, knowing deep down in the parts of her where dark thoughts grew that, *yes*, yes she knew it would end like this. One day.

Just please, not today. I'm not ready. We're not ready.

Panic detonated inside her as she drew the door open, the blast tearing away the walls separating Emily from her husband, dissolving the heat of the infection that was turning him into something he was not, revealing all of the raw memories she had of the man she'd married. A man whose face dimpled when he smiled, who despite his stubborn streak, despite his inability to remember that the toilet seat should go down and not be left up, she adored.

Love had stitched them together, made them whole; something better and more unique than anything either one of them had been before they met. But everything was different now. The stitches were being yanked from their skins, and the pain of coming unsewn was without comparison. Everything she'd come to think of as white had turned out to be black after all. Everything that was cherished had to be despised if she was going to stand a chance of surviving. And the joy of life had been replaced by a desire for it all to just end. There was no ugliness like loss, and now, as the front door to their home burst down and those thudding feet crashed in the hall, she knew that ugliness was about to reach a new low.

Not now. Please. Just one more day. One more day.

And through all this, a question.

How?

The corridor outside her bedroom was full of men with guns and head-mounted torches. They reached out and grabbed her, hands snaking about her arms, mouthing her name, and she found herself answering. They pushed her against the wall, knocking photographs off their hooks. Shadows and light, a ballet of figures skirting through her house like crazed dancers about a bonfire, shrieking prayers to a deaf sky.

Papers were flashed in her face. Photographs of her husband from his social media accounts. Sneaky surveillance shots of Emily in her pajamas putting out the trash. Of Lucette playing on the front yard. A warrant. She watched, unable to move, as the man in front of her moved his lips. They were linked by a chain of gummy saliva. There was no air in the room anymore. They had come and steeled it all away like fire. A fire that was spreading down the hallway, forcing doors open as it went.

There had been no pain that compared to Jordan's turning. Emily had felt lost at sea, tugged this way and then that by dueling currents, whilst from below reeds snatched at her ankles and dragged her down; and the more she flailed the more entwined she became. Now there was light in the water, shimmering and indistinct, lights mounted on heads screwed into bodies covered in clothes with the Ministry's insignia woven into its fabric. Stitched in. Not with love, but with diplomacy, with good intentions. Mercy.

I knew this would happen, came a voice from the darkest part of her. *And at the sad, strange end of the day maybe I wanted it to.*

But how? How did they know?

Perhaps the sky was not so deaf after all.

Sally.

Her daughter was screaming, carried away by silhouettes. Emily fought against those who held her, desperate to reach Lucette. Her small face, so shocked and sleepy in the glare of a torch.

Emily called out to her, reached through the human barricade, and still heard nothing. The current was strong down here. She longed to go back to her room and grab the machete from under the bed.

A cluster of men dragged Jordan out into the hall and wrestled him to the floor. He kicked out, his thin arms waving, but Emily knew he was too weak to fight them off. She ached for him then, felt the final strands that stitched them together being cut by these intruders.

They dragged Jordan across the tiles in the direction of the broken front door, his underwear bunching around his thighs as his skin screeched across the tiles. He looked so white in the glow of their torches, a child's chalk sketch of a man on a pavement moments before the rain came and washed it all away. His upturned feet slid from view, thumped across the threshold.

"Let me go," Emily assumed she was saying, yet still couldn't hear. There were tremors in her throat from her vocal chords, the thud of her pulse in her temples. That was all. The man in front of her, the one with the strands of saliva linking his lips, continued to bark at her, a hot diamond of spittle flying through the air to land on her cheek.

Emily clenched every muscle in her body and drew strength from her reserves. She'd heard stories of mothers overturning cars after accidents to get at their trapped children, stories of people running through burning rooms to retrieve family members—a primeval force locked away, accessible only through an extreme need to protect all you held close. And Emily had the key.

She kicked out, whirled her arms, connecting. Thud. Grunt. Torches went wide, gifting her with a few evanescent moments of shadow in which she ducked low and bee-lined straight for the door the intruders had hauled her husband through. Emily didn't stop to savor her assault, there was no time for that. She had to get outside. Now.

The moment her foot stepped through the architrave, lights trailed in on her. More arms vined about her torso and yanked her down the steps. Everything turned sideways—the moonlit front yard, the driveway—as the men and women of the Ministry forced her onto the grass. Dirt on her lips. Oxygen vanished from her lungs, and she didn't care.

Jordan was kneeling by the mailbox before black

skittish outlines of men holding guns. There was no color out here. Everything was monochromatic, a wartime photograph, a captured beat of history depicting the final seconds of a life before the inevitable execution. Her husband twisted around in search of someone to hear his pleas, the accordion contours of his ribcage casting their own shadow.

It played out in silence for Emily. Her hush—it felt both delicate as moth's wings and as steely as the stars staring down at them. She feared nothing would break it.

Jordan turned and locked eyes with her.

(*And reached across to take her left hand, slipping the ring on her wedding finger. His grin, so big and toothy, prickled his cheeks in those schoolboy dimples. What a goober, she'd thought, he's crying. The ring slid across her skin, snug-as-a-bug-in-a-rug, as her mother used to say. They were knit together now, legally and in the eyes of all those with them in that cramped southern church. And to prove their worth, they cheered when he lifted her veil to kiss her, just as they'd rehearsed—a goodish, respectable mingling of pecks and just a flick of the tongue.*)

He extended his arm out to her.

(*And then dragged Emily into his warmth. There in the cold hospital room they basked in disbelief so pure it boggled their minds. They had created life, made something from absolute nothingness. And now they held that life together, a girl. "What should we call her?" Emily asked, offering her breast to the baby. Her nipple tingled under the tug of those lips, the sensation rippling her skin in gooseflesh. He then whispered his suggestion in Emily's ear, and they laughed, nodding.*)

Jordan's button eyes blinked away the last of his humanity. The smile stretched across his face revealed the elongated curve of his teeth. There was sorrow there, so much loss, and Emily could see it, despite his inability to sculpt emotion through muscle and skin anymore. She saw him grieving for the final tie binding them together, and recognized it because she grieved for it, too.

Jordan spoke. And for the first time since the Ministry crashed through the gate, she heard.

"Emily," he said.

Emily.

One of the silhouettes put the barrel of a shotgun against his hairless head, haloed his face in a ring of torchlight. A trigger was pulled. Where there had been a face there now was a bowl of gruel and bone spears, the blood and gore streaking the mailbox. He toppled to the ground and was filled with flashes, bullets spearing him from every angle.

Like sound, like oxygen and pain, color crept back into the world then. That hue, regardless of the knowledge she'd housed in that part of her where dark thoughts grew, still surprised her.

The color was red. Devilish fireflies in the night.

RED

"**WHAT IN THE** name Sam Hill was that?"

It was the first time Emily had dropped the expression in years. When times turned south, so too did her vocabulary—even her accent sounded stronger. But the shock of her slip was nothing compared to the sound reverberating through the facility, ringing in her ears.

You know what that was, said a voice in the back of her head. *You know only too well.*

Woods was next to Emily at the door to her supervisor's office, surrounded by the five Crowners. As expected, their visitors had arrived in their 'casual' attire, a thrift store patchwork of summer shirts that made them look like unassuming RV drivers, only instead of prowling highways they coursed the corridors of America's hospice system. Like Emily and Woods, they had all flinched and ducked at the gunshot, exchanging wide-eyed glances.

A second blast rung out. Someone started screaming for help. Mykel.

"The break room," Woods said. She clutched her blouse, a gesture that undermined the ferocity of her tone.

"No, don't go," said one of the Crowners, a skinny man in a Hawaiian shirt. "We don't know what's happened down there. It could be anything."

Emily watched the stern-faced woman named Geraldine, whom she'd seen before (*Lordy, you don't forget someone like that*), drop the forged consent form and followed the echo, a hound sniffing out blood. Woods attempted to settle the other startled Ministry workers, men and women who had been drawn up from their offices at random, as Emily broke into a run, matching Geraldine's strides one for one. Her supervisor's yells ended with a scream for someone to call the goddamn police, and Emily sensed Woods' presence at her back again. Right where it should be.

Adrenaline pumped through Emily with such vigor that she didn't even bother to glance around the break room as they passed to check on Lucette. The moment she entered the space she sensed her daughter's absence and was grateful for it.

Woods forged ahead and threw the courtyard door open. Cold air slapped their faces, turned their breaths into shock crystals that fell across their boots.

The rational world was crumbling outside.

Mykel was on the ground, lying on top of the old woman who had approached Emily on her first day at the hospice, the one who told her that the dead roamed these halls. However, as bizarre as that sight was, it was nothing compared to what lay in the snow next to them.

At first Emily thought it was her husband, his skull cracked open in twilight once more. Only no. It *couldn't* be. The Ministry no longer exterminated the infected in their homes, dragging them out into the streets and slaughtering them like dogs as they had her husband. In fact, Jordan was the last person to have his life prematurely ended that way in all fifty states. It was his death that led to the revolt, catching the entire country off guard. Emily had been proud of South Carolina then, despite their betrayal coming from those very streets—from people she had trusted no less. The zombie may have bitten the modern world, but it was Charleston of all places that bit back.

At the time, Emily hadn't had the strength to join the revolutionaries, as those who had and hadn't known her husband threw Molotov cocktails through storefront windows, flipping cars so the President would listen. And the President did. It was from those flames that the hospice system was funded, the Ministry reconstructed, and statues erected around the country to commemorate what was now referred to as 'the atrocities'. Emily had taken her daughter, the little girl she did not blame for being what she was, and headed north up Interstate 85. Natalia her doll, however, Emily left on Sally's doorstep with an accompanying note.

You've earned this, it read.

So no. It wasn't Jordan on the ground in the courtyard. Understanding this didn't make the revelation any easier.

Because it was her.

Mama Metcalf. Flat on her back. A grotesque piece of art on display for all, only the artist, unsatisfied with her expression, had wiped away her face. Gone. As simple as that.

Emily didn't realize she'd been screaming until she

ran out of breath. The door slammed shut behind her and a siren blared. Someone must have smashed the emergency alarm in the break room, likely one of the five Crowners.

Mama Metcalf at Christmas dinner, smiling over the food she had made for them, pointing out her festive decorations, laughing as they watched the ball drop just last night, telling stories about Dick Clark, who Lucette had never even heard of—these memories faded, replaced by Woods as she ran forward with two of the Crowners, Geraldine and the man in the Hawaiian shirt. Thankfully, Mykel had the old woman immobilized, but from the bulge in her side it looked as though he'd busted a few ribs in the process.

Serves you right you hateful bitch.

Emily wanted to help in some way, but Woods yelled at her to step back. "Give us space, damn it!" Emily shuffled to the door, hands on her stomach, kneading the emptiness in her that Lucette had left behind the day she was born. Some holes were never filled.

Geraldine picked up the gun. She walked to the corner of the courtyard, looking up at the jacket thrown over the barbed wire fencing.

Woods pushed Mykel off the writhing old woman and sat on that busted ribcage herself. She proceeded to punch the intruder right in the face. Woods let out a war cry that chilled Emily to her core. The old woman flopped against the blood-splattered snow, unconscious.

"Excuse me, little dove," Geraldine said, easing past Emily to get back inside. Her tone was even.

Emily assumed the Crowner was well accustomed to disassociating herself from slaughter. Had to be.

The puzzle pieces started to fit together in Emily's mind. The old woman had somehow gained access to the courtyard and shot Mama Metcalf. Yet this realization didn't usher in any resolution because it didn't feel real, more like a movie.

The only thing that rang true was a single thought, a single repeating word:

LUCETTE. LUCETTE. LUCETTE. It chimed with the alarm.

"I have to find my daughter," Emily told Woods, who stood over the old woman, fist raised. Her breaths were coming hard and fast. "I have to leave you."

The one remaining Ministry worker, Mister Hawaii as Emily thought of him, was still out in the yard. "I'll stay with her," he said, kneeling beside the beautiful black woman who had so intimidated and challenged Emily on her first day of work.

"Go," Woods said to her, eyes rabid beneath her brow. "Where there's one motherfucking terrorist like this there may be more. Make sure Lucette's safe. If she's not, do what you have to do. Got me, girl?"

Emily grabbed the door handle, clenched it tight. "Crystalline."

She rushed into the building. The break room was lit with red lights cast from wall sconces. In addition to this, every door in the building would have automatically swung shut as a protective measure against fire threat. Closed—not locked. The sprinklers hadn't turned on, and of that Emily was relieved. If that had happened, some of their patients (*not guests!*)

may get wet, and pneumonia was a constant threat in the winter months.

"Lucette!" she called, though the room was small enough to see that there was nobody in it. Emily took a step and her shoe crunched shards of glass from the BREAK IN THE EVENT OF EMERGENCY alarm near the door. She kicked them aside when she saw the open book of origami on the dining table. And then she knew.

She just knew.

Emily headed toward Corridor 3, passing the occasional co-worker who tried to stop her and find out what was going on. "Protect everyone and brace for evacuation," she told them. Woods was right; this cowardly act of violence may be a sign of things to come. And worse, the protesters had been so riled up that morning. Sometimes all it took was a single drop of blood in the ocean to send the sharks into a frenzy.

"Hey, New Girl!"

She stopped short of the door leading to the FSU and turned in the direction of the caller, thinking to herself that you needed a code to gain access to the ward, but her daughter could be too damn resourceful when she wanted to be. Mykel ran up to her, blood slushing down his face in rivulets.

"I'm coming with you," he said, catching his breath, reaching over her shoulder to punch the code into the keypad. "You just never know." Mykel's presence confirmed that sick feeling of dread in the pit of her stomach, the suspicion that she would not *only* find her not-so-little-girl in Robby's room—but something else. "I'm just being realistic," he added, stepping in front of her and pulling the door open.

Emily grabbed his arm. His skin was slick with Mama Metcalf. "Thank you," she whispered.

Inside, she heard her daughter screaming. The sound was oddly muffled. Emily's heart started trip-hammering as she made a mad dash down the hall, following the red silhouette of her co-worker. To her right she was vaguely aware of the blur of bare skin in Tammy's room, but she didn't pause to investigate. Lucette's squeals were getting louder and more desperate—and yes, they *were* coming from the direction of Robby's room.

"No, no, no, no!" she cried.

Keep her safe. Above all else. Keep. Her. Safe.

The two nurses hit a hard left and pivoted into the room, their shoes squeaking the linoleum. Emily feared she would freeze up again as she had out in the courtyard.

Robby had Lucette in his arms, his teeth clamped on her lips as the girl fought to free herself. Blood was gushing down on the sheets creating Rorschach patterns spelling death—her daughter's if she didn't break free of this paralysis right now. The air thickened, time slowed, everything ran at half-speed.

Mykel made it to the bed first and grabbed Lucette's arm with one hand whilst smashing his other fist into Robby's face. The boy released his hold on the girl and snapped his teeth. Mykel jerked back to avoid the bite, yanking Lucette with him. The girl pirouetted on the spot and landed against her mother's chest.

Hysterical yelps tore from Lucette, the bottom half of her face gore-streaked. Her lips had been torn clean off. Eyes wide with shock as she reached up to finger the parts of her that were no longer there.

On an instinctive level, Emily knew that the only thing that was truly important in her life had been whisked away. But fear, that elemental need to survive, cauterized the wound. Gripping her daughter's arm so tight their flesh might as well have been fused, Emily hauled Lucette to the door, forced her through, looked back.

Robby leapt over the side of the bed, landing on the floor. He was uncoordinated and ungainly, as all infected were right after the change, but he was *fast*. A blood-splattered lick of lightning that could have struck anywhere on earth, yet which had settled on this very room. On them.

On Mykel.

It wasn't Robby that attacked him. All remnants of the boy's humanity were gone as he scurried at the man Emily had found so intolerable. The child was an 'it' now. One of them. A smiler. A grotesque thing worthy of the mob's hatred.

"Run!" Emily yelled to her daughter. "Get out of here. I'm right behind you."

The girl didn't need to be told twice. She made her way down the corridor, a ball bearing in a pinball machine, directionless, pained and scratching at the seeds of her infection. Emily spun to the room and watched Robby leap on Mykel, forcing him against her shoulder. The three of them fell in the corridor and onto the hard floor.

Snarling rat teeth snapped inches from their faces. Its black eyes didn't blink. Not once. It wouldn't stop until it had them in its jaws, their blood in its gullet, digging for their marrow. Mykel drove his knee into the boy's stomach, flipping him off, gracing Emily with just enough time to scramble away.

"Go! Go! Go!" he yelled.

The smiler rushed at them again, scrambling like a lizard, snarling and slobbering. It reached the end of its IV tubing, the needle coming free and spurting morphine across the floor. The stand overturned and clattered against the mattress.

Mykel was on his hands and knees, trying to force himself upright when the smiler leapt on his back, the gown flapping away in the process, revealing the former child's mutated form. Skeletal protrusions. Mismatched muscles. The elongation of its fingernails and teeth.

Screech. Screech. Screech.

Lucette collapsed at the foot of the door leading out of the FSU before having a chance to open it. Seeing her there, Emily had to make a choice. She either helped Mykel or she helped herself. In the end, the smiler cast this decision on her behalf. It slung its head sideways and latched its jaws around the base of Mykel's neck.

Emily scuttled for the wall, reached out to balance herself, only to misjudge the distance. She tumbled onto her knees—blinding white bolts of pain—and doubled over.

She watched, almost at the point of disbelief, as the thing that had once been the boy she pitied lived up to its *other* moniker. The bone-eater.

It forced its arms and legs on Mykel's limbs, pinning him down, and then ripped the nurse's head into an unnatural hinge with its jaws. A human Pez dispenser. Only instead of candy, the prize was a fountain of blood jetting up over the opposite wall. The boy lifted a hand and used those elongated nails to slit open the flesh of Mykel's back. Then the creature arched itself rearward, contorting itself almost double. The head was still in its maw as it peeled Mykel's spine from his body. It all came away from the flesh in one fluid motion, swinging through the air like a ball on a chain.

The bone-eater dove on its bounty. Ate.

Emily regained her footing, alerting the creature to her presence again. She ran, hearing the clatter of bones as it discarded the severed spine in search of fresher specimens. Its greed was inexhaustible.

The door at the end of the corridor was *open*. Lucette was dragged from sight.

Emily moved faster than she'd ever moved in her life. Scratching fingernails against linoleum at her heels. She dove through the FSU architrave where Speedy and Tammy were pulling Lucette from harm's way, about turned, and flung the door shut. The old man dropped his shoulder against the metal barricade as the smiler tried to force it open from the inside. It was a fire-escape safety measure that security doors automatically unlocked when the alarm was sounding. Both she and Mykel had forgotten this when he punched in the code earlier.

"You. Have to. Escape," Speedy said through elongated teeth as he wrestled with the weight.

Emily picked Lucette up again, her back and knees crying havoc. "Come with me," she said to Tammy, who was crawling back over to the FSU entrance, her gown open to reveal her bed-sore spotted buttocks.

The infected woman reached the door and stretched out her arm as though casting a blessing. "No. It *won't* take us! RUN!" That command blurred with the whine of the alarm until there was only one ear-piercing squawk that Emily feared would never end. Were she to survive this, she was sure it would loop in her head forever in both waking and dreaming lives, twin reflections of each other where monsters lurked. Emily held her bleeding daughter, and even though it hurt like hell, turned her back on her saviors, two people who had come here to die with dignity and in the end discovered it on their own.

Emily limped to the fire exit and pushed it open, clear light shining through, forcing their shadows back into the hall like sacrifices to the creature. Snow crunched underfoot as Emily emerged into the day and kicked the door closed.

***

Tammy had been right—the creature had no taste for tainted goods and passed them by. It was inevitable that their depleted strength would be no match for it, and only moments after Emily and Lucette had spirited themselves away and along the side of the building towards the rear entrance to the car park did it break free of the FSU.

It carried itself with the elegance of a dead ballet dancer, arms swishing through the air so its elongated claws whistled as it walked. The whiteness of its skin was reflected in every door handle, in the concave mirrors masking security cameras, upturned in a teaspoon thrown from a dropped food tray. Hunger drove it on, sending it stalking through the corridors of the hospice. Were it unlucky in its pursuit, it would go back to the other place and suck the fluid from the bones it had collected before.

The creature wore an apron of blood, ready for its next meal. If given the choice, it would eat but one bone from a hundred living things over every bone from a single person.

***

Woods stood up, spent. The old woman at her feet had stopped breathing, despite her efforts, despite hating herself for even trying. Not even her up-to-date CPR training had saved her, regardless as to whether or not survival was warranted. Woods wiped the dead bitch's stinking spit from her own mouth.

The one remaining Crowner joined her, the skinny man in the Hawaiian shirt. He grabbed his arms, trying to warm himself. "You did everything you could," he said, shivering.

Woods tried not to cry. That would come later. "Maybe I did. Maybe not. Let's get back inside and find the others."

Before closing the door on the courtyard, Woods saw Mama Metcalf's unmoving legs splayed in the snow. That woman, as annoying as she could be sometimes, had deserved a better end than the one she'd met. Woods said a quick, silent prayer, hoping that the big southern girl didn't freeze her ass off on her way up to the Pearly Gates.

***

Thirty simple seconds tick-tocked on by, and despite the electric crackle of expectancy in the air, Mama Metcalf remained well and truly dead. Even her blood had stopped flowing, ruby diamonds on a cigarette-butt strewn patch of land. The old woman across from her, Wanda Mabry, would also never move again. Her index finger was curved inwards as though still depressing an invisible trigger that shot invisible bullets of hatred at a sky that would never die.

Sirens sung in the distance. When the hospice alarm was activated an automatic call out was prompted to the fire brigade. They would be there soon. Though not quite soon enough.

A chirping issued from this crimson scene.

It wasn't a bird, although in many ways it sounded like one. It came from the old-fashioned cell phone that had tumbled into the snow beneath the staff picnic table during Mykel's tussle. The screen had cracked in the fall, but the name of the incoming caller was clear as day.

Two words flashed over and over.

MY ERIK.

***

Woods and the Crowner in the Hawaiian shirt rounded the corner into the corridor that would lead, after two subsequent turns, to the front of the building. Their hands were plastered over their ears to block out the alarm, but Woods still heard him ask, "When do you think the police will get here?"

She didn't have a chance to answer. It was as though someone had reached inside her throat and snatched the oxygen straight from her lungs.

One of the other five Crowners, a bearded man wearing a long sleeved plaid shirt—as though he'd set out that day to fell trees as opposed to felling a life—sat against the wall. A tossed aside play thing. His hands were upturned to the ceiling; a wedding ring glimmered scarlet from a nearby sconce. Beyond the

shock of seeing him, Woods felt a throbbing for the people he left behind. The slaughtered man was loved by someone somewhere, a person who likely at one point or another sat him down and held that very hand, pleading as spouses do, "Are you sure you want to work at the Ministry? What if you get called up for Crowner duty? I'm frightened for you, babe." And now here he was. Head slouched to one side. A husk, having been emptied out. Ribbons of intestines arranged before him in tribute to the fickleness of his flesh and the merit of the bones that had been thieved.

The door to the room next to the dead man opened a fraction, and in the red light Woods saw a woman's face. It appeared engraved in the dim. She was one of her guests. Her name, from memory, was Margaret, though Woods couldn't be sure. There were so many of them, a revolving door of infected souls passing through this way station. Men, women, and children coming from terrible places with terrible histories heading straight into the great big black on the other side. Woods' jolt over seeing the dead Crowner was secondary to the guilt of not being able to recall that woman's name with certainty. Such was the curse of caregivers, the most diminutive cuts bled the worst.

"You have to leave," the shadowed face whispered. "Quick. Before it gets you. It'll gobble you up. *Fee-fi-fo-fum.*"

Maybe-Margaret's hand—so youthful—snaked out into the hall and pointed back in the direction from which Woods had come. "It went *that* way. Fly out the front door before it's too late. Fly!"

Woods shuddered, fearful she may vomit. Maybe-Margaret's door clicked shut with unnerving delicacy.

A tiny clunk. Woods felt alone, exposed. She turned to calm the skinny Ministry worker who, God bless him, had been by her side since the courtyard. Ha—calm. The truth of it was that Woods was downright terrified and longed to hold his hand, to have this complete stranger squeeze her fingers and tell her that everything was going to be okay.

Only he was gone.

Woods stood there, frozen to the spot, the siren continuing to boom about her. She sensed movement just around the corner they had come from, only she was too terrified to retrace those few feet to identify its source. The faces of her children, her darling boys, boiled in her brain like bones in a pot. She wanted to see them again. Hold them. Devour them with love and bathe in their broth.

A gurgle split the air. Snapping. The hairs on Woods' arms, unwilling dancers to sounds she didn't want to hear.

Close. Too close.

It was coming from right *there*.

Woods felt every muscle in her body grow tense, focused on the sensation. The fear was in the marrow she longed to keep. Clenching her jaw, she took two steps backwards, her shoes squelching against something wet—an intestine popped under her heel, splattering shit. The stink was raw. Her exhale was soft but determined; Woods had no desire to die today.

Crunch. Schlop.

The boy snapped its head around the corner, dead eyes honing in. Its smile was so wide it almost extended off the sides of his—*its*—face, like a child's crayon drawing, the kind her sons used to make and that she'd bring into her office and plaster across the walls. She watched it lurch further into view, blood and licks of hair glossing its body. A wet mess fell from its hand, forgotten in its desire for something new.

Something from *within* her. A part *of* her. Something ripped from Woods' body.

No, she said to herself. *It's mine. Always.*

Woods snapped to and sprinted towards the entrance to the building. Doors opened on her left, on her right, the peekaboo faces of the infected men and women emerging from the dark of their rooms to scream at her.

"Run!"

"It's going to get you!"

"FASTER!"

She rounded the final corner and saw daylight at the end of the red—she could see through the two glass doors at the lobby leading to the street. Outside. Possible safety. In the mix of this light she saw the mob swarming. They were still waving their placards, only now in addition to their number there were members of her staff there, too. She had trained them well; that was their evacuation point in the event of an emergency. The '*unlikely* event', as it had always been phrased, on account of things like that never happened in places like this.

Woods heard the bone eater coming after her.

She kept on running, doors slamming shut on either side as she went—*thump, thump, thump, thump*. Despite this, she could still hear them cheering for her, banging against their walls in the hope of successfully making a distraction. Even though it wasn't working she loved them all for trying.

Woods propelled herself further, arms swinging hard and fast.

The corridor seemed to stretch out in front of her, yanked away like pulled taffy, shrinking the exit down to a pin-sized vanishing point ahead. Only 'ahead' didn't quite fit right. That suggested her destination—her survival—was within reach. This wasn't the case. Woods had coursed this stretch of well-worn linoleum a thousand times over and never once had it seemed so long. So far away. She was learning now how fear made all things malleable. It melted the strong to make them weak. It warped walls and time alike, heaving them to their absolute limit.

Feet slamming. Her panting, her screams. The light grew brighter.

It was with her, reaching out to snatch at her hair. She didn't dare look back, but caught sidelong glimmers of its white skin reflected in the port windows of the doors as she sprinted on. Woods screamed when it mewled, the heat of its breath on her neck.

(fee-fi-fo-fum)

She was close to the first glass door. Faces turned in her direction. They pointed. Signs dipped. Steam-bursts from the O's of their mouths at the sight of her running towards them. Towards her dead end.

Because in order to get through the first door into the antechamber Woods would have to stop to either swipe her pass (which was sitting on the desk in her office) or punch in the manual code. That would take a few seconds, plus a handful more for those old pneumatic doors to grind open. The bone eater—*no, he's a boy*—the smiler—*he's a boy, goddamnit*—the fucking zombie—*there I said it!*—would be on her in no time at all.

He was that fast.

Woods had never expected it to end this way. She thought she would live to see her boys have children of their own, to see the world evolve into a better version of itself. People said she was a Grade A bitch, and Woods wouldn't deny that, but nothing gained was forged without fire. And God help her, she was a full-time burner. Always had been. Like Mama Metcalf, Woods thought the few remaining good people on this planet deserved better than *this*.

She saw it now.

I'll die against the glass door, fumbling at the keypad. Slaughtered in view of my staff and the spiteful crowd of protesters who come here day after day like flies on shit. The zombie will rip out my spine and eat my marrow. And then what will all those people say? Well, I know that only too well.

See. I told you so.

"DROP!" came a voice from her right. So quick and well measured, a shadow sidestepped into the hall from where it had been hiding in the room just before the door into the reception area.

***

The black woman dove to the floor at Geraldine Leonard's feet, revealing the blur of teeth and claws at her back. This locomotive of hunger pummeled at her now, faster than any of the outlawed clichés she'd grown up with as a child from movies and literature had led her to believe. Her mind struggled to comprehend its viciousness. Logic kept her firm, kept her legs locked in the A-frame position, kept her eyes sharp.

Rationality came to her rescue. The creature was just a reanimated corpse, and one of the many things Geraldine had over the creature were the reflexes of the living. That, and the crazy old woman's gun.

A crown of a different kind.

There was no time for Geraldine to offer up a prayer. Not even a quick one. But as far as she was concerned, she'd banked up enough amens in her lifetime to last her a while.

There was a job that had to be done and an ugly one at that. That was why she was here. That was why she hadn't killed herself long ago, in spite of the sin. She was a Crowner, and in some ways always had been. It was all she had left.

Geraldine pulled the trigger.

***

Betty Hopkins was by her husband's side near the front of the crowd watching the action play out within the hospice. Back at college she had, of all things, been a drama major—her aspirations of being an actress crushed under Tim's thumb. Now it was as though she were watching herself up there in this impromptu theatre. Betty was always running, just like the woman behind the glass doors. The only difference was when Betty ran she never seemed to move anywhere.

And the blur at *her* back? She didn't like to overthink as to what—or who—that was.

The staff closest to the building screamed. They scattered down the steps in their direction. Betty felt Tim pushing against her, easing her out of the way. The sign that he'd given her earlier, the words, KILL ALL BONE EATERS—THE NEW BIBLE: VERSE 1 scrawled across it, slipped from her hand.

A gunshot rang out from the foyer.

Betty glanced up, the crowd around her breaking apart, leaving her alone at the foot of the building's steps. A creature that in many ways reminded her of her son flung against the first interior glass door, chest first. Its exploded shoulder was on full display for them to see like a living specimen in a jar.

No.

The thing up there didn't just look like her son. Good God in heaven—it *was* her son. Of this she was sure. A mother knows, even mothers who never wanted to be mothers in the first place.

Before she had a chance to wonder how all this could be happening or why, a shadow materialized from the red glare behind the thing that used to be her Robby. He spun around then, his bleached skin shimmering in the winter sunlight. Betty told herself that her son hadn't seen her, though on some level she suspected he had, and not known who she was.

It's okay, Robby. I don't know who I am, either.

Another gunshot on the stage, another blaze of light. Robby's head detonated against the door in a mosaic of brains and cracked glass.

Betty dropped to her knees, all sensation in her body gone now. The curtain closed, draining all color from the day. She looked around for her husband and found him in the crowd once more, his face almost indistinguishable from those of the others—except for the I'VE GOT MOXIE cap. What was it about a common cause that made everyone look like everyone else? Hatred devolved people somehow, she thought. Made them legion. She saw them standing there, still and silent, and none more so than her husband himself.

"See Tim," Betty Hopkins said. "You all got what you wanted."

THE CHOICES MOTHERS MAKE

LUCETTE WAS FINALLY sleeping.

Emily sat by the girl's bed, listening to her labored breathing. It was so deep it made the bedsprings squeak. All about them were bundles of soiled tissues, cotton buds, a half empty bottle of gin, red bath towels that had been drenched red. The prior afternoon and the night that followed had been its own kind of slaughter, not so different from that which she'd witnessed at work. Emotional destruction.

These had been the most difficult hours of Emily's existence.

She patted her daughter's sizzling forehead, trying not to look at the bandages wrapped around the lower part of her face. The wet fabric sloshed inwards and outwards with every one of her daughter's desperate intakes of air. This detail broke Emily's heart because it made it all seem too real. And it *was* real, despite the way the hours since leaving the hospice had blurred together, like those fitful times when dreaming and waking mingled. A blur of wishing versus truth, giving up versus the *fear* of giving up. There had been so much screaming, especially in the dark. The girl had been hysterical, her pain coming in waves, and fearful that the noise would attract neighbors, Emily had no choice but to silence her.

Yet another bruise on her kewpie-doll face.

The clouds that had brought so much snow lately had broken, and early-morning sunlight poured through the window, liquid gold. This did nothing to temper the darkness of Emily's mood, however. In fact, the light almost seemed to be God's way of mocking her.

No. Not God. That prick doesn't exist.

Whatever doubts she'd had over this before were confirmed now. The scar of this was only too real.

She'd been holding back the tears since they'd left the hospice the previous day, trying to be strong so as not to upset Lucette any further, but now that she was out cold, Emily slumped to the floor, drew her forehead to her knees, and gave in. These convulsions wracked. She still hadn't changed out of her scrubs, which were splattered with drying blood. Only she hardly noticed this. Snot mixed with the red in a medley of bodily fluids. It felt good to let go.

The crying juiced her of the prior night's memories. They slipped through her fingers in the shape of tears to patter the floorboards between her knees. It was the great purge, and the venom of what had happened had no choice but to come out.

Holding a pillow over the side of Lucette's head as she thrashed against the dining room table. Pouring gin over her lipless mouth to sterilize the wound. "Christ, fuck, lie still!"

Watching her girl loll between consciousness and unconsciousness. The way her eyelids jittered this way and that with the terror of her first night fever.

234

They would only get worse as the infection incubated.

Tying Lucette to the bed with scarves so she couldn't hurt herself. Struggling to make the knots tight enough, cautious of cutting off circulation to those small hands.

Blood absorbed into the fibers of towels, blooming like daisy-chain flowers growing up through Chicago snow.

Begging for Lucette to be quiet, locking her in her room with all the toys that Mama Metcalf had bought for her at Christmas. Emily sitting against the door as her daughter scratched at the wood behind her, moaning. Moaning. Moaning. Emily lifting her head to see a rat scurry through the kitchen. It scuttled away and into a hole she'd never seen before. It was there, under the sink cupboard. Emily longed to shrink herself down to the size of a thimble, just like Alice in her world of Cheshire cats and looking glasses. Then, and only then, would Emily crawl inside that dark warren in the wood. Perhaps the rat that would not die, would eat her until she was dead, and maybe that would be a good thing.

The quietness from Lucette's room. Emily wondering if the girl had slipped away.

Leading Lucette into the bathroom and peeling off her soiled clothes. Bathing her skin in soapy water. Holding her as three words kept running through her head: keep her safe, keep her safe, keep her safe. Whilst all around them the shadows in the bathroom turned into hands that stretched out to snatch away the only thing Emily had left.

To take that which had been claimed.

"Don't leave me," Emily had said. "I don't know how to be alone."

The same stitching that had bound Emily to her husband was the same as the one linking her to her daughter. It was fraying before her eyes.

Sitting by the window and watching the night outside. Praying that dawn would come; afraid that dawn would come. Wondering if anyone had noticed that the world had devoured them, and if they had, wondering if those people gave a shit.

Looking at the knives in the kitchen drawer.

Emily wasn't sure how long she stayed like this, but the ringing of her cell phone penetrated through. She stood, dizzy, and hurried from the room, not wanting the ringing to rouse the sleeping girl. In the hallway, she pulled the cell from her pocket and stared at the screen.

It was Woods.

Emily was surprised the call hadn't come sooner. But with all the commotion and confusion at the hospice, there had doubtlessly been more pressing matters to which the administrator had to attend. It didn't occur to Emily until later that seeing her boss's name on the incoming call display meant two things: One, that Woods was alive, and two, someone *had* noticed that she'd been devoured.

Someone *did* give a shit.

The ringing droned on. Like the bandaged rasp of her daughter's breathing, answering would only make this situation more real. There was so much more hurt to be experienced and the first lashing would no doubt come from the voice on the other end of the line. Emily told herself to be brave, and wished that the dead had a way of crossing phone wires like they sometimes did in the movies, and that when she answered it would not be Woods talking. It would be Mama Metcalf telling one of her obtuse asides. Or maybe her own mother, that southern lilt like cold water on a scalding burn.

Taking a deep breath, Emily slid her finger across the screen and held the phone to her ear. It was hot. "Hello," she said, astonished by how steady and *normal* she sounded considering the circumstances.

The same could not be said for Woods. "Emily, thank God. Where the hell are you?"

"I'm at home."

The rat was peering out of its burrow at her again. "Why'd you leave, girl?"

"I did what had to be done. Just like you said. I grabbed Lucette and went."

"I understand that, truly I can. You probably did the right thing. Everything went—" Emily listened to the crackling phone line as Woods searched for the appropriate word. "Sour."

"I'm sorry I left," Emily said. "I know protocol in situations like that is total lockdown. To not leave."

"You're safe. That's what matters. But the police are going to want to question you. If you don't come in today they'll come to you. The Ministry will be here, too. We need to follow their advice on how to proceed. I'm in way over my head."

Emily found herself fumbling for an excuse to stay out of it. "I really didn't see much. By the time I got to the courtyard Mykel had already subdued the woman who—

Killed Mama Metcalf.

She couldn't quite bring herself to say the words aloud. With everything else that had happened, and her concern for Lucette, she hadn't spent much time dealing with the fact that her friend was dead. It was too much to take at once; Emily would have to push this aside to be dealt with later.

Assuming, of course, that the knife in the kitchen drawer remained in its place.

Snug-as-a-bug-in-a-rug.

"It doesn't matter how much you did or didn't see," Woods was saying. "This is how it goes. Bring Lucette, too."

"She was terrified by the whole thing. I've only just got her down now. Our night was fucking awful. It'll have to wait, okay?"

"Well, I don't know if it can. Because of what happened with Robby, everyone in the facility has to have a thorough physical examination to ensure there's no threat of contamination."

"Lucette wasn't anywhere near the FSU," Emily lied.

"Em', *help* me to *help* you. Both of you." Another stretch of silence, broken by a couple of half-stifled sobs. "I need you here. Please. You're the best I've got. You always were."

Emily disconnected the call and turned her phone off.

There came more scurrying from the kitchen. Tiny teeth chewed through something rotten, something damp.

The warmth of gin dribbling down Emily's throat was followed by a *clunk* as the bottle drummed the floor. A line of small sugar ants marched across the kitchen tabletop. "Hello," she said, crushing them under her thumb. "Hello. Hello."

Five tabs of Aspirin in the palm of her hand. Bitterness as she ground them between her teeth. They didn't stay down long. Her vomit was green.

The pipes behind the walls groaned as she showered. Bloodied water swirled between her toes. Emily giggled because she thought it looked too red. As though it were fake.

Dressing herself. Cold sunshine on her face whilst she brushed the knots from her hair. Ouch.

Time didn't exist in the apartment anymore. The clocks didn't tick.

She saw Robby scuttling across the floor when she blinked. Covered her eyes. Removed her hands. *She saw Lucette scuttling across the floor now, bald and hungering bones.*

That whisper again: *Keep her safe. Keep her safe. Keep her safe.*

Emily returned to the kitchen. The rat was gone but the knives were still there.

She stood inside the doorway to Lucette's room. The girl lay on her back, one arm thrown over her eyes. The scene might have been picturesque, a moment to capture for the photo album, were it not for the fact that her mouth was bound in blood-encrusted bandages.

There came a knocking at the door.

The icy hand of fear gripped her throat, throttling breath. Had Woods sent someone after her, were the police waiting on the porch to take her and Lucette in?

Or was it Sally again, coming to fish for clues from her daughter and her silly stuffed toys so she could run off and report them to the authorities? Perhaps Sally had already done this—been listening to them through the walls, maybe the rat was her spy—and it was the Ministry out there with their shotguns. Locked and loaded.

No. They don't do that anymore, remember? Jordan was the last.

The bat that Emily had given her daughter for Christmas leaned against the wall. She snatched it up and, closing the door behind her, tiptoed toward the front of the apartment.

Knocking again.

With a trembling hand, she reached out and undid the latch. If Emily got through this, she thought she might dig out the suitcase she'd pre-packed, the one she'd hidden under the bed in her room in the event it all came tumbling down. Though as to where she would escape to, Emily hadn't a clue.

But until then, there was only the bat in her hand and the door swinging open on a squeaking hinge. Her knuckles turned white.

They were all there waiting for her.

Mama Metcalf and her busted open head, dripping gray matter down the folds of her scrubs. Jordan's face over her shoulder, his dimples as prominent in death as they were in life. The thing that used to be Robby slithered at their feet, its wide toothy smile was just for her. Mykel lurched across the lot in blind arcs, spurting gore as he went from where his head and spine were not so long ago housed. Her parents were there too, each with their matching heart-attack guts swinging before them, stinking of the earth they were buried in. They weren't alone. The knockers at her door were there by the thousands, dribbling over one another, clambering for fresh bones to suck the marrow from.

A generation of the dead looking for somewhere to die.

Emily ran at them, bat—

(machete)

—raised. Her grunts were muffled by flying scalps, dried dust blood clouds. Her daughter's present snapped jaws from necks, sent eyeballs flying into the sky in nightmarish home runs. Emily swung, over and over again, granting them all the relief they so desperately wanted, until she was doused red from head to toe. Her own private genocide.

Corpses piled high through the lot, snow falling on them in straight lines. Chicago's rats scurried out from the nearby streets and made burrows from their slashed necks and crushed skulls. Emily looked down at the corpse at her feet. It belonged to Lucette. She hadn't been bludgeoned to un-death by the bat she'd asked for Christmas that year.

No.

Her head had been sawn off with one of the kitchen knives—

The front door banged against the wall with a thud, revealing the empty threshold.

Emily panted, still holding the baseball bat tight, poised to attack if need be. There was nobody out there. Not Sally, no random UPS man, no concerned neighbor having overheard moans and yells in the night. There were no Ministry members, either. No Woods.

Just flat snow leading from the porch.

Her grip loosened and the bat bounced against the WELCOME mat. Emily slammed the door shut and put her forehead to the paneling, crying. "Help me," she said to nobody. "Help me."

And then there was more knocking.

It hadn't come from the front door as she'd at first thought, but from inside Lucette's room. Emily knew what had to be done.

A surge of anger coursed through her as she held her daughter on the bed. Anger at Lucette for breaking the rules, for putting herself in harm's way. Anger at herself for bringing her daughter to the hospice and exposing her to all this danger in the first place. Anger at Woods for granting permission for Lucette to be there, and anger at Robby for dying at the wrong fucking time. Anger at the old woman who had climbed the fence, creating the distraction the universe needed, angry at a God she didn't even believe in for not being real.

It all left her drained and exhausted. This grief was unlike any she'd ever experienced before. And Emily had experienced more than her fair share.

She brushed the hair from Lucette's sweaty forehead, speaking her name.

The girl murmured and snuggled deeper into her mother's chest. Emily was persistent, however, the longer she put this off, the harder it would be.

When the girl opened her eyes, tears spilled from them to dampen her bandages. Emily watched those small fingers reach up and tenderly draw down the veil cast across her jaw, uncovering the sinewy flesh around her mouth. This grotesquery robbed the girl of the ability to pronounce most words.

"Ang eye goin' to die?"

(Am I going to die?)

Every annunciation proved itself an agony.

Emily took a deep breath and decided nothing would be accomplished by lying to the girl at this point. "Darlin'—

(oh, god this hurts)

—yes."

The girl's tears continued to flow. *"Ing how horry, angnny."*

(I'm so sorry, Mommy.)

"Shh," Emily said. "No sorries. No sorries. It's not your fault, or anyone's."

"Angnny?"

"Yes, baby?"

"Ill I ee alone like Owgee?"

(Will I be alone like Robby?)

"No," Emily said, firm, placing a hand under the girl's chin and forcing their eyes to meet. "I'm going to be right there by your side, darlin'. I'll never ever ever leave you. I'm your Mama. I'm going to be with you every step of the way. Every goddamned step. Together. Together always. Always."

Lucette frowned, winced with pain. *"Huh?"*

Emily closed her eyes, took a few deep breaths, and then returned her gaze to her daughter. "Bite me, Lucette."

The girl recoiled from her mother, horrified. She moaned protest.

"Oh, I know, baby. I know. But that's why I want you to do it. You *have* to!"

The girl scurried off the bed and into the corner, crouching on her haunches. *"Onghhhhh—"*

Emily joined her daughter, sliding down the wall to sit next to her. She took the girl's hands. "Be brave for me, honey."

"Owww. Owwwww. Owwwwwwwwwww."

"You are my life, Lucette. You always were. I'll keep you safe. You won't ever be alone."

The girl pulled her hands away and touched the place where her lips used to be. *"It urts hoe utch."*

(It hurts so much.)

"I know," Emily said. "But they'll take care of you. They'll take care of us both. Together. Together always."

Lucette squeezed Emily's hand and sniffled. "Hangilly."

"What, honey? I don't—"

"Hangilly."

It dawned on Emily then what her girl was saying. The word settled like lead.

(Family.)

Emily rolled up her left sleeve and held out her arm. Tears threatened again, only she forced them back. This was the right thing to do, the only course of action. She had no idea where the energy to muster this bravery had come from—she'd been so close to giving in and taking the knife from the drawer—but that strength was there. Perhaps it always had been.

"Now, Lucette. *Now!*" Hating herself for this cruelty but needing to be strong, she slapped the girl across her damaged mouth, eliciting a scream. Emily joined her, holding out her arm again. "Do what Mommy tells you."

THE END?

Not quite . . .

Dive into more books by the authors:

Flowers in a Dumpster by Mark Allan Gunnells—The world is full of beauty and mystery. In these 17 tales, Gunnells will take you on a journey through landscapes of light and darkness, rapture and agony, hope and fear. Let Gunnells guide you through these landscapes where magnificence and decay co-exist side by side. Come pick a bouquet from these Flowers in a Dumpster.

Tales from The Lake Vol.2 anthology—Beneath this lake you'll find nothing but mystery and suspense, horror and dread. Not to mention death and misery—tales to share around the campfire or living room floor from the likes of Ramsey Campbell, Jack Ketchum, Edward Lee, and of course Aaron Dries.

Tales from The Lake Vol.3 anthology—Dive into the deep end of the lake with 19 tales of terror, selected by Monique Snyman. Including short stories by Mark Allan Gunnells, Kate Jonez, Kenneth W. Cain, and many more.

If you enjoyed this book, I'm sure you'll also like the following Crystal Lake titles:

Sarah Killian: Serial Killer (For Hire!) by Mark Sheldon—Follow foul-mouthed and mean-spirited Sarah Killian on an assignment from T.H.E.M. (Trusted Hierarchy of Everyday Murderers), a secret organization using serial killers to do the dirty work for their clients. Sarah's twisted sense of humor alone makes this Crime Fiction/Horror/Thriller a worthy read.

Gutted: Beautiful Horror Stories anthology—an anthology of dark fiction that explores the beauty at the very heart of darkness. Featuring horror's most celebrated voices: Clive Barker, Neil Gaiman, Ramsey Campbell, Paul Tremblay, John F.D. Taff, Lisa Mannetti, Damien Angelica Walters, Josh Malerman, Christopher Coake, Mercedes M. Yardley, Brian Kirk, Stephanie M. Wytovich, Amanda Gowin, Richard Thomas, Maria Alexander, and Kevin Lucia.

Run to Ground by Jasper Bark—Jim Mcleod is running from his responsibilities as a father, hiding out from his pregnant girlfriend and working as a groundskeeper in a rural graveyard. Throw in some ancient monsters and folklore, and you'll have Jim running for live through this folk horror graveyard.

Blackwater Val by William Gorman—a Supernatural Suspense Thriller/Horror/Coming of age novel: A widower, traveling with his dead wife's ashes and his six-year-old psychic daughter Katie in tow, returns to his haunted birthplace to execute his dead wife's final wish. But something isn't quite right in the Val.

Tribulations by Richard Thomas—In the third short story collection by Richard Thomas, *Tribulations*, these stories cover a wide range of dark fiction—from fantasy, science fiction and horror, to magical realism, neo-noir, and transgressive fiction. The common thread that weaves these tragic tales together is suffering and sorrow, and the ways we emerge from such heartbreak stronger, more appreciative of what we have left—a spark of hope enough to guide us though the valley of death.

Devourer of Souls by Kevin Lucia—In Kevin Lucia's latest installment of his growing Clifton Heights mythos, Sheriff Chris Baker and Father Ward meet for a Saturday morning breakfast at The Skylark Dinner to once again commiserate over the weird and terrifying secrets surrounding their town.

Pretty Little Dead Girls: A Novel of Murder and Whimsy by Mercedes M. Yardley—Bryony Adams is destined to be murdered, but fortunately Fate has terrible marksmanship. In order to survive, she must run as far and as fast as she can. After arriving in Seattle, Bryony befriends a tortured musician, a market fish-thrower, and a starry-eyed hero who is secretly a serial killer bent on fulfilling Bryony's dark destiny.

Wind Chill by Patrick Rutigliano—What if you were held captive by your own family? Emma Rawlins has spent the last year a prisoner. The months following her mother's death dragged her father into a paranoid spiral of conspiracy theories and doomsday premonitions. But there is a force far colder than the freezing drifts. Ancient, ravenous, it knows no mercy. And it's already had a taste . . .

The Dark at the End of the Tunnel by Taylor Grant—Offered for the first time in a collected format, this selection features ten gripping and darkly imaginative stories by Taylor Grant, a Bram Stoker Award® nominated author and rising star in the suspense and horror genres. Grant exposes the terrors that hide beneath the surface of our ordinary world, behind people's masks of normalcy, and lurking in the shadows at the farthest reaches of the universe.

Little Dead Red by Mercedes M. Yardley—The Wolf is roaming the city, and he must be stopped. In this modern day retelling of Little Red Riding Hood, the wolf takes to the city streets to capture his prey, but the hunter is close behind him. With Grim Marie on the prowl, the hunter becomes the hunted.

Children of the Grave—Choose your own demise in this interactive shared-world zombie anthology. Welcome to Purgatory, an arid plain of existence where zombies are the least of your problems. It's a post-mortem Hunger Games, and Blaze, a newcomer to Purgatory, needs your help to learn the rules of this world and choose the best course of action.

The Outsiders Lovecraftian shared-world anthology—They'll do anything to protect their way of life. Anything. Welcome to Priory, a small gated community in the UK, where the only thing worse than an ancient monster is the group worshipping it. Is that which slithers below true evil, or does evil reside in the people of Priory? Includes stories by Stephen Bacon, James Everington, Rosanne Rabinowitz, V.H. Leslie, and Gary Fry.

Eden Underground horror poetry by Alessandro Manzetti—Another snake, another tree, another Eve. A surreal journey into obsessions and aberrations of the modern world and the darker side, which often takes control of the situation. Winner of the 2014 Bram Stoker Award for Superior Achievement in Poetry.

If you ever thought of becoming an author, I'd also like to recommend these non-fiction titles:

Horror 101: The Way Forward—a comprehensive overview of the Horror fiction genre and career opportunities available to established and aspiring authors, including Jack Ketchum, Graham Masterton, Edward Lee, Lisa Morton, Ellen Datlow, Ramsey Campbell, and many more.

Horror 201: The Silver Scream Vol.1 and *Vol.2*—A must read for anyone interested in the horror film industry. Includes interviews and essays by Wes Craven, John Carpenter, George A. Romero, Mick Garris, and dozens more. Now available in paperback, as well.

Modern Mythmakers: 35 interviews with Horror and Science Fiction Writers and Filmmakers by Michael McCarty—Ever wanted to hang out with legends like Ray Bradbury, Richard Matheson, and Dean Koontz? *Modern Mythmakers* is your chance to hear fun anecdotes and career advice from authors and filmmakers like Forrest J. Ackerman, Ray Bradbury, Ramsey Campbell, John Carpenter, Dan

Curtis, Elvira, Neil Gaiman, Mick Garris, Laurell K. Hamilton, Jack Ketchum, Dean Koontz, Graham Masterton, Richard Matheson, John Russo, William F. Nolan, John Saul, Peter Straub, and many more.

Writers On Writing: An Author's Guide—Your favorite authors share their secrets in the ultimate guide to becoming and being and author. *Writers On Writing* is an eBook series with original 'On Writing' essays by writing professionals. Be sure to check out the webpage regularly for new releases.

Or check out other Crystal Lake Publishing books for your Dark Fiction, Horror, Suspense, and Thriller needs.

CONNECT WITH THE AUTHORS

Author, illustrator, and filmmaker **Aaron Dries** was born and raised in New South Wales, Australia. When asked why he writes horror, his standard reply is that when it comes to scaring people, writing pays slightly better than jumping out from behind doors. He is the author of the award-winning novel *House of Sighs*, and his subsequent books, *The Fallen Boys* and *A Place for Sinners* are just as—if not more—twisted than his debut. ChiZine Publications, Samhain Horror, Crystal Lake Publishing, Scarlet Galleon Press, and a number of international magazines and online venues have published his fiction and art over the years. As a filmmaker, Dries' short films have garnered awards in Australia, the UK, and the USA, and he is currently hard at work on multiple feature screenplays as well as novels. Feel free to drop him a line at aarondries.com or contact him through Twitter and Facebook. He won't bite. Much.

Mark Allan Gunnells loves to tell stories. He has since he was a kid, penning one-page tales that were Twilight Zone knockoffs. He likes to think he has gotten a little better since then. He loves reader feedback, and above all he loves telling stories. He lives in Greer, SC, with his husband Craig A. Metcalf, and blogs at http://markgunnells.livejournal.com/.

Hi, readers. It makes our day to know you reached the end of our book. Thank you so much. This is why we do what we do every single day.

Whether you found the book good or great, we'd love to hear what you thought. Please take a moment to leave a review on Amazon, Goodreads, or anywhere else readers visit. Reviews go a long way to helping a book sell, and will help us to continue publishing quality books.

Thank you again for taking the time to journey with Crystal Lake Publishing.

We are also on . . .

Website
http://www.crystallakepub.com/

Books
http://www.crystallakepub.com/book-table/

Blog
http://www.crystallakepub.com/blog-2/

Newsletter
http://eepurl.com/xfuKP

Instagram
https://www.instagram.com/crystal_lake_publishing/

Patreon
https://www.patreon.com/CLP

YouTube
https://www.youtube.com/c/CrystalLakePublishing

Twitter
https://twitter.com/crystallakepub

Facebook page
https://www.facebook.com/Crystallakepublishing/

Tales from The Lake Anthologies Facebook page
https://www.facebook.com/Talesfromthelake/

Writers on Writing Facebook page
https://www.facebook.com/WritersOnWritingSeries/

Beneath the Lake Videocast Facebook page
https://www.facebook.com/BeneathTheLake/

Google+
https://plus.google.com/u/1/107478350897139952572

Pinterest
https://za.pinterest.com/crystallakepub/

Tumblr
https://www.tumblr.com/blog/crystal-lake-publishing

We'd love to hear from you.

With unmatched success since 2012, Crystal Lake Publishing has quickly become one of the world's leading indie publishers of Mystery, Thriller, and Suspense books with a Dark Fiction edge.

Crystal Lake Publishing puts integrity, honor and respect at the forefront of our operations.

We strive for each book and outreach program that's launched to not only entertain and touch or comment on issues that affect our readers, but also to strengthen and support the Dark Fiction field and its authors.